The Entwined Past

The Entwined Past

Once was a quiet town, until?

Feven Ghebre

Published by Tablo

Published in 2022 by Tablo Publishing.

Publisher and wholesale enquiries: orders@tablo.io

20 21 22 23 LSC 10 9 8 7 6 5 4 3 2 1

INTRODUCTION

This is the story of three young women who discovered each other in a town, become best friends, and together unravelled the mystery of a city hidden deep within.

Elena Richards is an eighteen-year-old brave and humble girl who is more than willing to fight for what she believes in. Her mother, Victoria, a sweet woman of forty-eight, recently died in a car accident. Ever since she died, Elliot, Elena's father, has been drinking tremendously and doesn't seem to be able to grasp life anymore. Elliot is fifty years old and a miserable, angry older man. After witnessing this, Elena is unable to take any more pain. There have been instances where her father has physically abused her and acted aggressively towards her. One morning she made up her mind; she wanted to leave; she did not want to go to school that day; her dad had already left that morning, so this was her chance. After quitting her part-time job, Elena arrived at the house where she grew up. It is an older two-story house with white windows and three bedrooms. Her bedroom is purple and is down the hall from her dad's room. Elena walked into her bedroom, packed her belongings and left. She took her wallet, bank card, and a few snacks. As she walked to the bus station, she decided her next stop is Craven Heights. That evening Eliot came back to an empty house. He did not care. He popped open another bottle of whiskey, sat on the couch with his feet up, and went on about his miserable day.

Mariah Talen and Derek Charlise were married for two years. Mariah is twenty-one years old, and Derek is twenty-nine years old. The two of them were a power couple before what happened to them. Derek is a marketing professional with an unprofessional attitude; he is tall, snarky, has a warm skin tone, and has a copper hairstyle. Mariah is a very charismatic artist with a very charismatic personality.

In addition to being a hardworking and dedicated woman, she is also a pretty woman. Her light brown hair and dimples look perfect on her. Mariah and Derek live in is the east side of Port Sunfield. The apartment they live in is located in a quiet part of the town. The apartment consists of two bedrooms, a living room, a dining room, a kitchen, and a bathroom. Mariah decided to go for a modern style. Derek, a businessman, is having difficulties balancing his work and personal life.

Derek and his wife were facing fertility issues, and due to this, Derek lost interest in Mariah and began to have an affair with his assistant, Clare. Clare is a twenty-three young woman with 5, 2, height and somewhat curly brown hair. Derek wanted a child so badly that he decided to cheat on Mariah to have one.

There was a time when Derek wanted a child so badly that he and Mariah started constantly fighting about it. The fighting led to cheating, and Derek cheated on Mariah. The affair resulted in Derek being away from home often. Despite all of Derek's efforts to hide it, he has to admit that it takes a toll on his mental and emotional health. His wife can sense the infidelity, which he denies every time she tries to confront him. But one night, the nightmare began for Mariah. Derek came home from work after a long day of work. First, he had some food; then he walked up to his bedroom. Mariah is lying on the bed reading, and then shortly after, she starts to make a move toward her partner. As soon as she makes that move, Derek moves away. He leaves the phone on the bed and then heads to the shower.

After five minutes or so, his phone starts to beep. Mariah could sense something was up with the phone. There was something in Mariah that told her to pick up the phone. As she picked up the phone, there was a message from Clare. As soon as Derek stepped out of the shower, everything crumbled around him. When Mariah confronted him, everything began to fall apart. The two of them got into a fierce argument. It seemed to Derek that he was never able to make Mariah happy no matter what he did. In his head, all he could think about was fertility, and how Mariah and he aren't a good match for each other. He felt that it is Mariah's fault that they can't have a child. It was at this time that something snapped in Derek. After hiding this affair for so long, Derek decided to release all the anger he had built up inside him. He took his hand, raised it and hit Mariah. Mariah was so taken aback by this that she ran away from him. When he came running to her, she slipped and fell down the stairs. Mariah was hospitalized for three weeks as she suffered from a broken leg.

However, after two months, she has fully recovered. The fighting and the way Derek hit her caused her to divorce Derek. Yet, he still keeps coming back into her life. He sends her text messages every now and then. While Mariah is working on herself right now, she is still shocked by what Derek has done to her. Currently, she is dealing with anxiety and depression.

Mariah works as a part-time staff member at a small coffee shop in her spare time and commutes to work every day by bus. One day, after Mariah left the shop, she went home, packed her belongings, and decided to make a change in her life. She called a taxi, and it dropped her at the nearby bus station. She went on her way to Craven Heights. It was something about the history of Craven Heights that made Mariah think it would be a good place for a fresh start.

Kayla Weber is a young woman of seventeen years who grew up in a rough neighbourhood. She is a brilliant, rational and kind person. The area she lived in had a lot of problems. The community was middle class, it was unsafe at night, and there were a lot of robberies. Her biological father died in a car accident, and her birth mother was a drug addict. Her Foster parents Greta and John found Kayla when she was five years old and adopted her. Her brilliant nature and excellent grades allowed her to undergo a summer writing internship at Craven Heights. Ella, her friend, even offered to have her sister Tori, who now lives in Craven Heights, stay with her. Ella is a sweet, adorable, funny, and beguiling eighteen-year-old girl with many talents. She is helping her friend out.

However, everything started to change when Kayla's foster parents began to be unkind to her over the months. It started with complaints about her bedroom not being how they liked it or clean. For example, the posters on the wall were of her favourite musicians. The parents were insulting her and were very hurtful to her. She was even slapped by her foster father. She wants to escape her nightmare, but she needs some help. Her boyfriend Jalen is a nineteen-year-old ambitious, very gentle and courteous boy. He will do summer placement in Port Sunfield, and then in September, he starts university in Port Sunfield. Since Kayla is turning eighteen in a few short days, she decided to leave her foster parents' residence and stay at a friend's house. After being verbally abused by her foster parents for years, Kayla agreed that when she turned eighteen; she would leave home. Now that the days have passed, Kayla is legally able to leave her home without any issue. Kayla walks up to her room, packs up all her belongings and leaves. Kayla fills in her friend Ella with everything that's been going on. So the following day at school, she decided to talk to her guidance counsellor about the writing internship in Craven Heights. The guidance counsellor agrees that it's a good idea. Kayla packs up her belongings at her friend's house, and Ella drops her at the bus station – Kayla takes the bus to the town of Craven Heights. It was a gloomy night in the city when the ladies boarded the Go Bus (departure 9:00 pm evening) on that grim night in town. The bus pulled up to the station and picked up the three ladies, Elena, Mariah and Kayla. The bus picked Elena Richards up around 9:30, wearing a sweater, jeans, and black boots.

Then the bus picked up Mariah Talen, who also booked the same bus. She is wearing black leggings, a bodysuit, and a t-shirt; she wears casual clothing. She is in a jumper that matches the colours of her hair followed by Kayla Weber, who is victorious, bright, and adventurous. The shorts and blouse that she is wearing are colourful.

The three women have never met, but they have all dealt with similar problems. While riding the bus, something terrible occurs. The bus suddenly breaks down. The girls are left sitting outside in the middle of the night. Almost everyone on the bus has already left. All of the people who rode the bus from work to home were random, working-class individuals.

The last stop was Craven Heights. The bus broke down just before Craven Heights. Each of them introduces themselves to the others. Everyone was trying to escape something. At this point, they had no idea what made them come close to each other. It was as if they were feeling driven to talk. The only thing they had in common was exploitation. However, they are all beautiful, young, passionate, atypical, and similar in many other ways.

CHAPTER 1

The day began like any other day. As the girls were preparing to leave town, they had no idea what would happen. Eighteen-year-old Elena Richard walked up the creaky stairs and into her bedroom; she packed all her belongings and put on jeans, a sweater, and boots. Then she walked with her backpack up to the bus station. As soon as Elena arrived at the bus station, she bought a one-way ticket. After gaining access to the station, Elena made her way to the location where the bus had left, which was in Port Sunfield. She had flashbacks of her past life as she waited for the bus. Elena hated what the drinking had done to her father and was not sorry about leaving. When she tried to persuade him that he should receive treatment, he refused, thinking he knew better than her. Due to all the fights between Elena and her father, Elena longed for peace and perhaps for a life where there would be no negativity in her life at all.

Even though the bus hadn't arrived yet, Elena decided to dash to the washroom as soon as possible. She runs there and does what she needs to do. She saw Aiden, a nineteen-year-old boy from her school, as she left. Aiden Enger is an old classmate. He is tall, medium-built with dark hair, and has an average appearance. Aiden's hair is in a neat bun as he smiles at Elena. Elena noticed Aiden as soon as she returned to the waiting room. She decided to go over and introduce herself to him. As it turns out, Aiden is one of the rebels at school. He has gotten countless suspensions and even detentions throughout his life. Elena was not surprised to see him out of school that day. As soon as Aiden remembered Elena, he talked to her about why she wasn't in school. She told him that he shouldn't make a fuss about it. Aiden doesn't know that Elena is running away from her vicious father, so Elena begins to open up to Aiden about her situation as time goes on. Although he came across as the " wrong boy" type of guy, Aiden looked cool. From that moment on, Elena liked talking to him, and from that point on, the time passed very fast, and then the bus to Craven Heights appeared. Then Aiden decided to get Elena's number to keep in touch with her, and so she gave him her number, and off Elena went to get on the bus to Craven Heights.

In the meantime, after the accident happened to Mariah Talen. She could not stop thinking about her husband's terrible behaviour. In the two months since Derek pushed her down the stairs, nothing has changed due to his actions. After getting a new job at a coffee shop, Mariah worked on herself. Derek still tries to contact her even though she doesn't want anything to do with him. After waking up in the morning, Mariah turns to her left, grabs her phone and checks the time. Then she walks to the washroom, brushes her teeth, takes a shower and combs her hair. After doing that, Mariah wanders through the apartment and into the kitchen; she makes herself something to eat. Now she is ready to leave her house for work. When she arrived to work, she had a hectic day as usual. When her job hours are over, she comes home, walks to the sofa, falls over on the couch, and begins reflecting on the day. When she contemplates her life, the only option she deems fit is to leave the town. Finally, she musters up the courage and takes a taxi to the station. The cab arrives at her apartment, and the driver picks her up. Mariah gets inside the cab and is dropped off at the bus stop. When Mariah arrived at the bus station, she got her ticket and waited for the bus to arrive. As she waits for the bus, another girl happens to be in a similar situation as Elena and Mariah.

Currently, Kayla Weber is a foster child living in a foster home. Unlike most foster homes, Kayla's place is huge and spacious. There are three bedrooms in the house. Among the three bedrooms is Kayla's blue room, which is cluttered and unorganized. Her foster parents are not able to understand her at all. This was true of her biological parents as well. That's why she has decided to stay with her friend Ella for the time being. Ella invited Kayla into her home and told her she could stay there whenever she wanted, as long as she wanted. After visiting with Ella for a few days, she decided it was time for her to leave. After all, Elena didn't intend to return. The only thing that makes her life worth living is her relationship with Jalen. It was going well between Kayla and Jalen; he started college in

Port Sunfield, their hometown. When Kayla discussed the internship opportunity with the guidance counsellor, she was looking forward to starting the internship in Craven Heights as soon as possible.

Seeing that the bus was leaving for Craven Heights, Kayla got out of Ella's car and headed into the station. She walks through the cold, gloomy station; she opens the door and walks to the ticket counter. Kayla gives the guy her ticket; he looks down, checks it, and gives her a pass. She saw the bus approaching, grabbed her belongings on the floor, ran towards the bus, and hopped on. The situation's dynamics start to change very quickly as soon as these girls board the bus. At first glance, it appears that they have something in common. Mariah and Kayla were the first to get on the bus, followed by Elena. At this point, the bus had been on the road for more than two hours. It wasn't until the bus halted that the girls grasped what was happening. A moment later, they realized what was occurring. They discovered the bus driver had announced just what they had anticipated.

CHAPTER 2

The bus driver lets everyone know that he's calling for assistance and that everyone should sit tight. The girls don't know what to do. After the bus driver spoke to the mechanic, he let the girls know that everything would be okay. The girls didn't seem happy about it. Hours went by, and it became a long cold night. The sky is dark and grey, the wind howling in the distance and the moon shining through the clouds. During the whole bus ride, Elena was the first to initiate a conversation with Mariah. The two girls have never met. However, they began to talk. One of the other girls, Kayla, was sitting by herself, writing in her journal, and was thinking about her boyfriend, Jalen, who she left back home. Even though she missed him, she knew he was doing big things in Port Sunfield. As for Kayla, she eagerly waits for someone to fix the bus. Kayla's phone began to ring; she got a phone call from her old friend, Tori. She picks up the phone and tells Tori she is all right and will be there soon.

Elena couldn't resist overhearing Kayla's conversation while talking to her friend. When she saw Kayla, she went up to her and asked her where she was going. For a moment, Kayla thought she was a bit weird. Yet, Elena insisted that Kayla get to know her since they were in the middle of nowhere. Because of the lack of anyone else to talk to, the girls began to open up to each other. In response, Kayla opened up to Elena. She told her why she was on this bus and what had happened to her. She felt sorry for her; Elena could also see Kayla was distressed. She wanted to share her experience with Kayla because she was in the same situation. As it turns out, Kayla and Elena have a lot of things in common. There was a car accident involving Kayla's biological father and Elena's mother, who died. That is something they have in common with each other. During Elena and Kayla's conversation, Mariah grabbed her bag, walked over, and introduced herself to them. Mariah had a similar story to share as well. And so Elena and Kayla were listening as Mariah shared her life story. They both listened intently.

She had difficulty sharing what had happened. Mariah's story was shocking for both Elena and Kayla. They could both relate to what she went through. She had trouble communicating what had happened.

Upon hearing everything she said, Elena and Kayla are shocked at what happened to her. Both Elena and Kayla can relate to what she went through. Mariah was glad she confided in them. They felt like friends to her. It seemed like everyone could use a friend. They talked and shared where they were heading throughout the night. Although they all were going to the same town, their paths diverged. Mariah goes to Craven Heights to get back into art and show her work in a gallery. Kayla will be doing an internship in Craven Heights. Elena intends to change schools and start fresh. All three have plans for a new start but are unaware that things will drastically change tonight. Their plans all included creating a new life in a new town. Elena had some leftover money from a part-time job in Port Sunfield. Kayla still had some money left over from Jalen. Jalen loaned her some cash since she started an internship in Craven Heights. Kayla informed Jalen that she would pay him back when she got paid.

Mariah had some money left over from working at the cafe. They each created a financial plan before they left. While the girls were waiting, a mechanic arrived and repaired the bus. Unfortunately, the bus is delayed by a couple of hours.

As the girls rode the bus, they began to think about what they wanted to achieve in their new home of Craven Heights. While moving to a new city, they wanted to accomplish certain things. In a few weeks, Elena had enrolled at Upper Lake High School. She was to start classes in September 2019. Kayla lives with her old friend Tori, who is working at Morgan Wonders. In addition to that, Kayla likes to hang out with Tori occasionally. Even though this is the case, she is not about to stop herself from meeting her new friends, Mariah and Elena. Mariah even found herself a small studio apartment and sold her paintings online and to art galleries. The future looks brighter for the three girls bound together by the past.

Their dark memories brought them together, but now they are using them to build a brighter future.

Now that several months have passed, it is June 2020. The girls have settled into their new life in Craven Heights, but their former life has now ended. The families they left back in town are trying to adjust to life without them. The ex-husband of Mariah, Derek, is still with Clare and has remarried. Elena's father is still drinking and has ended up in a hospital for a month. After the hospital, he has to go to rehab till he gets better. Although things are starting to look up for the girls, there is always someone who tries to put a damper on it. Kayla obtained her G.E.D while working at Morgan Wonders. She still keeps in touch with her boyfriend, Jalen. When Jalen began attending university in Port Sunsfield, he made sure to stay in touch with Kayla whenever he had time. After completing his summer placement, Jalen started university in Port Sunfield. As for Elena, she just recently graduated from Upper Lake High School. Elena did not make many friends; she focused more on her studies than on making new friends. But she did spend a lot of time with Mariah and Kayla. A few months after the coffee shop closed back in August 2019, Mariah decided to use the leftover money from the business to open a gallery in the town.

Based on the way things looked, the girls were all busy going about their lives until something unexpected happened. A bus approached Craven Heights at around 10 pm, and someone stepped out of it; it was Derek Charlise,

Mariah's ex-husband. You may be wondering now why he is in Craven Heights. He heard about the gallery Mariah opened up in this new town. He also knew that she used the money from the divorce and the coffee shop to open the gallery. The next day, she receives a call from her gallery asking her to come down to discuss a few things. She swiftly gets dressed, showers grabs a quick breakfast and heads to work as soon as possible. She finds Derek sitting in her chair. In an instant, Derek turns around, and Mariah is shocked. She yells at Derek to leave, but he doesn't want to go. As all of this happens, Kayla's friends Elena and Kayla do not even know that Derek is in town. Mariah and Derek are engaged in a dispute regarding the gallery. Even outside, people can hear them shouting at each other. Elena and Kayla decided to grab lunch with Mariah at her art gallery during this time, but they found Derek and Mariah fighting when they arrived. As soon as Elena and Kayla approached Derek, he stormed out. After a brief moment of silence, Mariah falls to her knees. Elena and Kayla ran over to her, asking what the matter was. She explained that Derek had heard about the gallery and wanted to make a small profit from it. Elena said he doesn't have a right to do that; you will fight him in court if he does that. There's no arguing that Mariah worked hard for her gallery in this new town, and they damn sure weren't about to let Derek Charlise and his new wife take it from her.

Both Elena and Kayla struggle to cope with Derek's wanting to take Mariah's hard work away. Elena was serious when she said she would file a lawsuit against Derek. The moment she saw him, Elena knew he was a jerk. Mariah feels tough and is confident that she can handle whatever he throws at her. After all, she knows she has friends who have her back. That means that Mariah won't have to worry about Derek. She will spend time with her friends while Derek is away. Mariah, Kayla, and Elena go to the nearest coffee shop to get a latte to drink. As soon as the girls leave the gallery, they walk to the coffee shop and order their drinks. Elena picks up the three lattes and sits down at the table. They all sit around the table for a long time, chit-chatting with each other. As usual, this afternoon has flown by very quickly. Afterwards, the girls drank their refreshments and left the cafe at around 3:00 pm. Then Mariah went back to the Gallery, Elena went to the convenience store, and Kayla returned to Tori's apartment.

CHAPTER 3

With everything happening with Mariah, it just so happens that Elena's father finished rehab and is sober. Elena finally had some happy news. The nurse from the rehab center found out where Elena was and contacted her to tell her the good news. Elena was delighted but still had flashbacks of her father's behaviour when he was drunk, so she still wanted nothing to do with him. As she was reminiscing about her father, she recalled something Elliot used to do. Elena recalled how he used to slap her and throw objects around the house. She was happy in this town with her new friends. Elena finally made a life for herself. She feels terrific, like a million bucks, but she still hasn't forgotten about Aiden, the rebel boy from her old school; she often wonders where he is and what he's doing. Her curiosity is caused by the fact that she thought he looked cute.

Elena then remembers he gave her his number, so Elena decides to call him. She went into her purse, grabbed the phone and called him. As soon as Aiden picked up the phone, they talked for hours; Aiden went on to get good marks, graduate, and even go to the university of Port Sunfield. Elena then remembers Kayla's boyfriend, Jalen Archwood, also in university in Port Sunfield. Elena asked Aiden if he knew Jalen Archwood, and Aiden told her he had heard that name before but didn't personally know him. Aiden is the same age and has seen Jalen around before. Elena thought, okay, to herself. When Kayla and Mariah found out about Aiden, they wanted to know all about him and Elena, and whether she liked him.

Like are they an item, does Elena like him? She went on to explain that Aiden is just a friend. They just left it at that. Nothing ever happened between them. It was like Kayla and Mariah wanted something to happen, but who knows? As for other news, Jalen Archwood is considering visiting Kayla very soon. It is a bit hard to understand his schedule until he graduates. Kayla is doing great at her internship; she gets paid, which helps her with rent. So she can stay with her best friend Ella's sister, Tori Neils, who likes to party feistily and has a great sense of humour. Tori is not known much to Elena and Mariah, but she has been Kayla's roommate ever since she moved into the city. Ella is the one who introduced the two girls. The girls have been through a lot in this town. Undoubtedly, Derek's meltdown isn't the only one everyone has thought it was. The girls have been through a lot in this town. It's no secret that Derek wants the gallery from Mariah. Mariah does not seem willing to give it to him without a fight, so Derek decides to leave town and leave Mariah in charge of the gallery for now. In any case, who knows if Derek Charlise is planning on coming back because it just so happens that strange things start happening in the town when Derek Charlise leaves. Among the weird things are the disappearances of young girls in the area. Not long ago, young girls, such as Elena, Mariah and Kayla, went missing around town. The town does not know where they are, and no one seems to know what happened to them. Someone has been kidnapping girls.

Also, the girls have noticed that the town has become very grim and quiet and that people often don't seem to be leaving their houses. Attempting to raise awareness about the situation, the mayor appeared on television and discussed the missing girls. Before moving to this town, the girls had no idea this was happening, so they had nothing to worry about at the time. As a once relatively peaceful and secluded town, their initial thought was why is this happening? However, they had never noticed anything unusual because the city had been so isolated. Teenagers have been disappearing in the area, and there is a maniac roaming around in Craven Heights. In the city, the lights flickered on and off, strange message calls rang out, and people looked lifeless at the same time. The skies turned grey, and more lost people posters appeared. The girls didn't notice before and were curious about what happened to these lost people. The girls were apprehensive and afraid, and at the same time wanted to know what was happening. Kayla thought that she would write about what happened during her writing internship. Mariah and Elena also agreed. It turned out that the girls were investigating a missing person case. It was a terrifying experience.

CHAPTER 4

The girls gathered at a large and spacious library in Craven Heights and explored the town together during the excursion. Upon reaching the library's doors, the girls open them and walk in. When the girls are reading some news articles and books around the dining table, they discover that it was a small village founded in 4500 BC. These girls thought this was a frightening story and wanted to know more, which led them to start digging further into the missing people, primarily missing girls. The first cases of kidnapped girls occurred back in the 1980s. The report says that girls as young as fifteen were disappearing.

There was a sense of unease in the town after the Mayor mentioned the missing girls. Nobody looked like they trusted one another after that. It was clear that many people were aware of what was happening because there was a pamphlet with information on missing girls everywhere in the town.

The news spread quickly around town. The girls were surprised but wanted to know more about what was going on. Mayor Kaiser Beckett attempts to keep the strange events in town under wraps as much as possible. Still, more and more people began to fear to disappear, so the Mayor's position was to ensure everyone was calm and safe. The people of the town, as well as the girls, were terrified. In their quest to find out what was going on around town, the girls made it their mission to discover why the Mayor tried to keep it low. The girls thought that this sounded abnormal. I guess they are going to find out in one way or another.

After that, the girls spent the next few days investigating Craven Heights. Kayla wakes up, yawns, stretches and gets up from her bed in the morning. While she is getting up, she sends Elena and Mariah a quick text. Both Elena and Mariah just woke up as well. Throughout the room, the aroma of cocoa filled the air. Mariah and Elena are in the kitchen pouring cocoa into their cups to start their day full of energy.

It looked like this day was going to be busy. They had a lot to do; Kayla had a story for her internship. It was a story that would solve the mystery of the town. During her training with Morgan Ashford, Kayla brought up this concept to her boss, and Morgan was blown away by her idea. At the time, Mariah was walking to the gallery to resolve a few issues. Since Elena had just graduated from high school, she looked for a job. Although Elena could apply to several universities, she wanted to get into work as soon as possible. Elena wanted to do this to avoid studying and going to college because she didn't want to do so. She wanted a job immediately after graduating high school.

As Kayla's alarm clock rings off, she receives a message from an unknown number, which she ignores. She thinks it could be a random caller. Kayla received a letter telling her that someone was watching her. This message freaked out Kayla, so she texted Mariah and Elena about it. The girls took note of this. After hours, Kayla prepares for her internship at this fantastic company in Craven Heights. Elena heads to Starbucks on the other side of town to get a pumpkin spice latte before heading to the gallery to assist Mariah. Luckily, Mariah gave Elena a part-time job at the gallery since she graduated high school. What a fantastic coincidence! Eleven months ago, these girls didn't even know each other, and now they're like best friends and work together. It's nice to see women supporting women.

Whatever was happening, the girls made it their mission to stop it. Somebody or something is trying to commit notorious crimes in this small, beautiful town. Young girls are escorted and led somewhere unknown. During the 1980s, flyers about missing women started appearing around town. Nobody noticed what was happening; no one thought anything of it until more missing girls began to disappear. Everyone in the city is frightened for their safety. Parents worry about their children going outside.

Nobody knows what to do to stop the strange disappearance that has taken place. As usual, the Mayor sits at his desk without doing anything. Media coverage of the situation is almost nonexistent. It is precisely why Elena, Mariah, and Kayla are worried about their futures in this town. They had been looking forward to a new beginning, but it seems their brand-new life in this town is causing a mysterious issue.

The girls decided to learn more about this town and the missing people. There was a desire to discover what was happening and why such things were happening. The girls, in this case, were highly interested in this issue, as they had just become town citizens and, as new citizens, they have a right to feel safe and secure in it. To do so, they should have a chance to learn more about the town and the events there. The girls decided to go home and think about it some more. After waking up the following morning, the girls decided to explore the town more. After all, they wanted to find out what was going on. Elena is still pretty freaked out about the text message she received.

CHAPTER 5

There is someone in the city responsible for the girl's disappearances. Someone decided to send Mariah a text message to scare her away. The girls decide to find out what is going on in town; Mariah reveals the unknown message to Elena and Kayla. The message said, " If I was you girls, I would stop searching for something you don't know anything about." The girls were digging into this case way too much. With everything, it did not work; The girls searched all over the town to find out what was happening with the missing girls. The girls decided to go to the library to do more research. They took a shortcut through the cemetery in Craven Heights to get to the library as quickly as possible. After walking through the cemetery, the girls noticed that a man was following them but would turn away and look at a headstone picture after seeing them staring at it. Once they had spotted the man, the situation took a turn for the worse. Mariah was in a state of shock. The girls passed by the man in the cemetery on their way home. The man in the graveyard resembled Derek as if they were the same. When Mariah saw how identical the man looked to her, she squealed. She assumed Derek was in town, but he wasn't. Someone else was there. The girls decided to wait for the man, then follow him out of the cemetery. After leaving the graveyard, he walks through an alleyway and into a coffee shop. They discuss that they should question him. Therefore, Mariah agreed to go and ask him. She was utterly shocked and enraged. At first, she thought it was a joke because Derek wanted the gallery, so he scared her, so she gave it to him.

However, Elena felt something else was going on. Kayla was thinking the same thing. So then Mariah walks into the coffee shop and sees Derek drinking his coffee. She went over to him and introduced herself as Mariah Talen. Suddenly, he gave Mariah a horrifying look. Mariah was scared, but she got the courage to tell him how much her ex-husband Derek looked like him. Mariah showed him a picture of her ex-husband Derek. After looking at the picture, he tried to act as if he did not know Derek. During this conversation, he mentions that his name is Darrius Rivers. He is a thirty-one-year-old man who is quiet, rather unconventional, and not like typical masculine men.

He said he is not related to Derek. But, Mariah did not believe a word he said. She knew that he and Derek might be connected. Otherwise, why does his face look like the faces of her ex-husbands? At this moment, Darrius's phone began to ring, and he seemed eager to pick it up, but he picked it up, answered the call, and a loud voice greeted him on the other end of the line. Since Darrius told Mariah he had to go, Mariah gave up now, but she still thought Darrius was hiding something from her. So she decided to leave Darrius alone this time. Darrius got up from the table and walked out of the coffee shop.

Upon returning home, Elena and Kayla thought this finding was wicked, and they should inform someone, like the Mayor, of what happened. Despite that, the Mayor did not do anything to address the problem. He only mentioned the missing females once. Kaiser didn't continue to show that he cared about the situation. He did not take what was happening seriously. The girls thought this was strange, and they began to suspect something was wrong. The girls decided not to tell anyone they had spotted in the graveyard. They also asked the Mayor to do more about the situation. As for Kayla, it was vital for her to capture the story, especially since she came to this town to start a new life, as both Mariah and Elena did. The weird things happening in town came as a surprise to all three girls. Would their lives have been different if they had not come to Craven Heights? They did not want to think about this since they had travelled a long way to start a new life in a new town. They were not going to be scared off by the strange things around town. The girls were able to do big things if they focused. They have a lot of potential to do great things in the town. The story of Kayla about the city is coming to life. Despite these challenges, she continues to research and write about her experiences every day while living in the so-called town of Craven Heights. Kayla's internship story focuses on spreading awareness about the missing people in town and spreading the word about the situation. The goal is mainly to give the missing people a voice.

CHAPTER 6

Several weeks have passed since the girls stumbled upon a Derek lookalike in the cemetery. The girls remained silent for so long because they wanted to keep what they were researching under wraps and collect more information about what was going on. They were on the edge of their seats. It was inevitable that they would want to dig deeper into this issue and Kayla decided to meet with the mayor. Mariah and Elena wanted to learn more about the girl's disappearance, so they gathered all the news articles and tried to connect the dots. Now, the girls could have gotten some help from the police, but there were only a few sheriffs in the town at the time, and there was little they could do without any evidence. The missing young girls seem to have been forgotten slowly by most people in the city in the end. Everyone thought that they were dead or something like that. That is so unexpected and so heartbreaking for the families.

However, the girls never gave up hope, as if they believed they had seen the light. They all came here for a fresh start in life, but they did not expect strange things to happen to them when they got here. Now that terrible things were happening, they decided to help the town themselves. They chose to be good citizens and to do something for the city. Elena, Mariah, and Kayla felt that this could also be something they could do in the meantime to give back to the town that helped them begin a new life.

After several days passed, the ladies began to investigate the city, the names of the missing girls, and the associate locations. They even decided to have meetups at the library regarding what was going on and how they should proceed with their investigation of the missing girls.

After being in town for a few weeks, the ladies have already seen a lot. They checked the internet to see if the stories had backstories. Elena, Mariah, and Kayla thought conducting this type of research was scary. Simultaneously finding out about the town was very sad because this town has as much history as it does. The strange things they found in the town were not something they expected to find, but they were eager to learn what was going on. The ladies thought that this town had been through a lot.

At 8:00 am, Elena Richards received a call from an unknown number. She picks up the phone from the nightstand on her left side. As Elena answered the call, she heard heavy breathing. Several minutes later, Elena received a text message from the unknown phone number, telling her to leave town immediately and stop digging into things she did not know. She called Kayla and Mariah to let them know what she listened to. But this wasn't the only strange thing going on. They remembered the lookalike of Derek in the cemetery. They wanted to know if Derek had a twin, so Mariah asked Derek about it. "Is there a twin?" she asked. Knowing Derek, this was a bad idea since he ignored Mariah's call; he sent her straight to voice mail. Elena remembered Aiden, her high school friend. After describing the situation to Aiden, he decides to come and help the girls.

What a sweet gesture! Aiden will be here soon. Elena was exuberant at the thought of seeing Aiden again - she had a little crush on him back when she was at school. It was clear that Aiden would help the girls with this mission, so until he came to town, the girls put everything on hold, just when they were going to do that. To make an appointment with the Mayor, Kayla decides to call the Mayor's administrator. Kayla wanted to discuss this with the Mayor since he was the one who brought up the girls in a TV interview, and that's what made them pay attention to the matter. As a result of the recent incident, Kayla wanted to know what the town's mayor was doing about it and if anything had been done. Such as helping the missing girls' families. The plan was for Kayla to sneak into the Mayor's office one day. She told Elena and Mariah that the mayor might have something to hide. The Mayor seems a bit out of sorts and suspicious. Mariah and Elena were not aware that Kayla's observation was incorrect.

Mariah and Elena had no idea that the Mayor had done anything wrong. They thought he was hot. But Kayla was ignoring the two of them. Of all the people, Kayla seemed to be the only one who had suspicions about the Mayor. Elena and Mariah continued their journey as usual. On Saturday, Elena and Mariah had to close the gallery for the weekend. Kayla went back to her office in downtown Craven Heights. There must have been a lot of work since she had to organize some papers for work.

Elena, Mariah, and Kayla went out for breakfast the next day. It was impossible to forget Darrius Rivers and his connection to Derek Charlise. Also, they found Elena's call suspicious because she talked of someone breathing. In Mariah's mind, it may have been Darrius or Derek calling and trying to scare them. Elena agreed. Kayla's eyes grew wide. They decided to keep this information to themselves until they found proof.

CHAPTER 7

Aiden is on the bed, lying down when he awakens from his sleep. Upon awakening, he begins packing his bags and informs Elena that he will be arriving soon. Several hours have passed since Aiden arrived at the bus station. The bus pulls up, and he gets on the bus and goes on his way.

Meanwhile, Elena and Mariah have just closed the gallery and headed home. Kayla is out with her friend Tori and is enjoying the day. The girls decided to meet at the library in the late afternoon. It is almost like the library had become a sanctuary for them. They were curious to know more about what had been happening. They had not forgotten the lookalike of the man they spotted in the graveyard. Mariah wanted to do more research because she believed Derek was hiding something from her. However, Mariah still wanted to keep her main issue on the missing girls.

The next day, Kayla had an important meeting with the Mayor. She went down to the Mayor's office before meeting with the girls to speak with Mayor Kaiser Becket. Mayor Kaiser Becket, a thirty-seven-year-old mysterious and very strict man leads the city of Craven Heights. His collar is embellished with a livery, and he is wearing a full black suit with a livery collar on his neck. Kayla walks over to him and sits on the chair. Mayor Kaiser turns his chair towards Kayla, and then the two begin talking. Mayor Kaiser wanted to know what brought Kayla to his office and why she was interested in the case of the missing girls in the first place.

Kayla explained her background and why she would like to help because the vanished women were young, like Kayla and her friends. And Kayla has made it her mission to find these women, dead or alive.

At the end of Kayla's speech, the Mayor got up, walked around his desk, and commanded Kayla to stay out of this situation. It was vital to him that she leave it to the police, and if she showed any interest in this matter, he would have her arrested. The mayor is nervous that girls are capable of digging up the information. He didn't like that the girls were coming up to him and telling him that they knew this and had proof that he was hiding something. Kayla was surprised by what the mayor said and thought this was very suspicious. Then she stormed out of the office and went on her way to the library, where the girls were waiting for her at the library. When Kayla got there, she had several things to say to them. Everything she told them became clear to them. Likewise, Mariah and Elena were stunned, and now they felt that the Mayor was concealing something from them. Mariah and Elena were also surprised, and now they felt the Mayor was trying to hide something from them. At that point, a bus arrived at

Craven Heights, and a guy with jet black long hair in a bun came out on the bus. It was none other than Aiden! he finally arrived. The first thing he did was call Elena. Elena picks him up and asks him to meet him at a small coffee shop. She then brings Mariah and Kayla along with her.

While the girls are getting ready to go to the coffee shop, Aiden checks in. Aiden finishes his business downtown and makes his way to the coffee shop, where he meets Elena, Mariah, and Kayla. Elena saw Aiden; she rushed toward him and hugged him enthusiastically.

As Mariah and Kayla watch, they laugh and introduce themselves awkwardly. In the conversation, Aiden becomes more and more comfortable with Mariah and Kayla. Aiden is interested in getting to know the girls. Elena informs Aiden that Mariah is Derek's ex-wife. As it turned out, Aiden had no idea that Derek's ex-wife was Mariah. As Aiden remembered Derek's name, he had heard of his brother Jasper before. Jasper is a twenty-six-year-old who is mysterious, stubborn, creative and impulsive. He is Derek's brother. Aiden tells Mariah that he bought some weed from Derek's brother, Jasper, a very long time ago, and Derek was actually in the car with Aiden as he purchased the weed. To explain what was happening, Aiden asked Mariah who was the lookalike of Darrius Rivers and Derek. As soon as Mariah mentioned the lookalike to Aiden, he wanted to know it. Aiden stated that he had never seen Darrius Rivers around Derek before. Derek's only brother is Jasper; he has never heard of another brother being around, so he knows Jasper is Derek's brother. It even mentioned that Aiden had seen Derek back home before. However, he only saw him with the Jasper guy. As far as Mariah was concerned, Derek hid and sold weed with his brother when they married. It is how Aiden became acquainted with Derek. But the lookalike of him is what confused Aiden. In Aiden's words, one Derek is adequate, and now you're telling me there might be a twin somewhere in Craven Heights.

So now that Aiden is in town, he works with the girls on finding out more about Derek's twin. Aiden decides to take the girls to the city library to meet together. The moment Aiden arrives at the table, he walks over to where Elena, Kayla, and Mariah are waiting. He greets them and sits down. Elena mentions to Aiden that Mariah called Derek to ask him about the lookalike, and Derek straight-up hung up the phone. Aiden starts to laugh; he was like that Derek guy who always seemed off. Elena asked Aiden to help with something, finding out more about Derek, like following him around. Both Kayla and Mariah urged Aiden to agree to this.

Elena asked Aiden if he would agree to follow Derek around town during the conversation. Aiden said this could be dangerous because he doesn't want to be associated with the wrong crowd. But Aiden decided to do it; he was like, I have nothing better to do. Aiden thought, why not? She also forgot to mention that there were some missing girls around town. The girls believe the missing girls and Derek might be connected somehow. Aiden somewhat agreed. He said he would look into Derek first and then click the dots to the lost girls in town. Everyone started to think, could Derek be hiding anything? Then again, maybe he is hiding something. However, as they continued to chat, Kayla came up with an idea. She was also suspicious that the Mayor told Kayla to leave and stay away from the matter. Kayla said she would try to get into the Mayor's office to see if she could find anything.

Elena and Mariah both thought she was brave and crazy at the same time. Elena whispered something to the effect of, 'How are you going to get into his office with a high-grade security system?'. Aiden laughs again as Elena punches him in the arm. Aiden shrugged. As soon as the plan was in motion, the girls went about their day. Elena and Mariah head to the gallery to prepare for an art event this week. Mariah is putting some art on display, inviting community members to attend. It's great to see Mariah is putting herself out there. So then Kayla gets a phone call from Jalen, her long-distance boyfriend. She hasn't told him what is going on because she does not want to worry him. Elena and Mariah thought that was sweet.

The girls don't know what they're dealing with, so Kayla decided she'd tell Jalen about what's going on until everything settles down in town. There's no way Jalen will show up in Craven Heights and surprise Kayla. However, that would be kind of cute if he did. Kayla ends the call and tells Mariah and Elena to see Tori at the apartment. As I mentioned previously, you don't know about this Tori Keils girl yet. Who is she?

Torii Keils is a twenty-year-old student who works as a dispatcher for 911 services. She is intelligent and witty, and she likes to have fun. Having moved to Craven Heights a long time ago, she decided to settle here after graduating from high school. She seems to like it here, and it was great that she helped Kayla out when she ran away. Tori has gotten closer to Kayla since she ran away. Kayla decides to invite Tori to the gallery event to meet her two best friends, Mariah and Elena. When Elena and Mariah finished setting up in the gallery, they went up to their loft to get ready. They don't know what will happen in the next hour, but it will be exciting.

CHAPTER 8

It had been a couple of hours since Mariah's Gallery show began, and she introduced herself to everyone who was there and thanked them for attending the showing.

There was a great deal of appreciation for Mariah's work in town. The pictures were gorgeous. Everyone seemed to be enjoying themselves quite a bit. All of a sudden, someone or something arrived at the gallery event. Immediately upon opening the door, a woman dressed entirely in black entered, covering both her face and body. As she made her way through the crowd, people stared at her and wondered who the woman behind the black veil was. Elena immediately noticed this and took Mariah aside. Elena sincerely asked Mariah if she knew who the woman behind the black veil was. Mariah was perplexed, just as everyone else was. Tori and Kayla found this odd and decided to mingle with other guests. After only a short while, Kayla and Tori noticed that this mystery woman was approaching them.

Mariah and Elena, on the other side of the room, are watching this unfold. Suddenly the mystery lady pulls down her mask and reveals herself to be Gretchen Wellsford. 'Gretchen Wellsford' is a fifty-two-year-old woman with a mixture of wisdom and timidity. She is described this way because she is a resident of Craven Heights and knows the town much better than anyone else. Both Kayla and Tori were confused as they approached the lady. I guess they didn't want to be rude. Mariah and Elena can see this playing out. Suddenly, Mariah gets a flashback while she is in the library. When the girls were in the library, this old lady worked there. It seemed like she spent most of her time organizing books in the back of the library. As soon as Mariah remembers her, she goes up to her and introduces herself to her. Then she welcomes her to the gallery. Gretchen seemed to be harmless. However, Elena and Kayla thought she was eerie. The long black veil that she wore added to the spooky effect. Mariah was adamant that Gretchen had thought this was a Halloween party, but it wasn't. It didn't take long for the girls to warm up to Gretchen.

Just then, another surprise at the party; Darrius Rivers arrived at the event. I guess he heard about Mariah's gallery opening and decided to show himself. The gallery event was first mentioned to Darrius through a fellow handing out flyers about the event. Mariah's idea was to put up flyers around town before she held the gallery event to attract people to the event. As Darrius walked into the room, everyone started to stare at him. Besides Gretchen Wellsford, it was also Darrius Rivers who was the focus of attention. During the event, Mariah and the girls wondered why that was happening. Why are people looking at Darrius as if he were some criminal? In addition, Mariah walked over to Gretchen and said, excuse me, so that she could speak to Darrius again. The moment Mariah steps up to Darrius, Elena and Kayla can see the whole conversation play out. Elena and Kayla didn't like seeing Derek look alike at the party. It has not been disclosed to them yet who he is, but they will find out soon enough.

In the evening, the girls interacted with everyone at the party. However, everything was dark and gloomy throughout the evening. The girls feel quite nervous after meeting Gretchen and running into Darrius again. Gretchen and Darrius couldn't ruin their evenings, so the girls decided to have a great time. The guests liked some of the paintings. One couple even bought a photograph. Mariah seemed to be a big hit at the party. It looked like a nice night, and everyone looked like they were having a great time. After a short while, the party ended, and everyone started to leave. Both Mariah and Elena cleaned up the place and left it locked up. Kayla and Tori went back to their building. It was now 2 am, so the girls decided to sleep.

The following day, at Mariah and Elena's place, Aiden texts Mariah and tells her that he found an article written several years ago. It was an article about Darrius Rivers. He learned that Darrius Rivers had been a criminal in a previous life and that he was living there at that time.

During his lifetime, Darrius committed several mischievous thefts. Finally, the police caught him and put him behind bars.

He was released on bail a month before the girls arrived in this town in recent months. The girls are now trying to piece together the puzzle. As Aiden finished telling the girls the story, they speculated that Darrius and Derek might have a connection since they look alike and have identical personalities. Nobody knows what is going on. But, Aiden said he would find out more about Darrius by following Derek. Even though the girls found Aiden's discovery eerie, they still liked what Aiden discovered. After that, the girls' day came to an end. Aiden stayed in town for the weekend, but he would be leaving on Monday to complete the tasks. When Aiden returns to Port Sunfield, he will keep a close eye on Derek Charlise and report to Mariah, Elena, and Kayla.

CHAPTER 9

The time is 7 pm in Port Sunfield, and it is wet and cloudy outside. Aiden makes his way to the bus station and grabs his luggage. When he gets to the parking garage where he left his car, he throws his luggage in the car and heads to his apartment. It's now 10 pm, and Aiden decides to sleep. Kayla's boyfriend, Jalen Archwood, decides to meet up with him. Aiden and Jalen met through Mariah and Elena. It also turns out that Jalen and Aiden both graduated from the same high school. Aiden can get in touch with Jalen through the phone number Elena gave to Aiden. From that point on, Aiden can contact Jalen. Aiden informs Jalen of what has been going on. Jalen eventually heard it from Kayla. Even though he is trying not to get worried for Kayla's sake, he is still upset that this is happening. Jalen then asks Aiden if he can help him track down Derek Charlise. During the conversation, Aiden told Jalen about this Darrius Rivers guy connected to Derek. Jalen mentioned that we would need to follow Derek around to discover more about Darrius. Jalen saw that the Mayor posted a video on YouTube about the missing girls; now, he knows more about the situation than before.

In the meantime, back in Craven Heights, the girls are getting ready for work. Mariah and Elena get up at 7 to go to work. Kayla calls Jalen to check up on him and decides to stay home for a while. Since Tori is a 911 dispatcher, she asked Kayla if she ever needed any help with anything she may need, and she made sure that she pulled some strings to assist Kayla and her friends. It was very kind of Tori to do that, Kayla thought. On the other side of the gallery, Mariah and Elena are frantically at work finishing up some last-minute details. What a great decision Mariah made to open her gallery.

Back in Port Sunfield, Aiden digs deep into Derek Charlise. He first follows Jasper, Derek's brother, through a dark alley and into the drinking hub. There he finds Derek and Clare sitting at the table with Jasper. It is Jasper who leads Aiden straight to Derek and Clare. Aiden tries to stay out of sight whenever he sees them, or else it wouldn't be good. Derek will not catch him as long as Aiden is close to the back entrances. An hour later, Derek decides to move. As Derek leaves the hub, he kisses Clare and says bye to Jasper as he gets up and leaves the hub. The next thing that Aiden is supposed to do here follows Derek and observe what is happening. Aiden follows Derek down the street through a dark alley and into this secret location. Aiden sees Derek walk into the area that looks like a small spooky house. He couldn't get a good look, but he saw Derek talking to this Asian-looking man in his fifties, and he then paid him, and the man gave him a bag with something in it. Aiden kept thinking something was in that bag. But he couldn't figure out what it was. Aiden walked backward and ran out of the alley before Derek came out.

Meanwhile, when Aiden makes it to his dorm, he calls the girls to tell them what he found. After talking to the girls, Mariah, Elena, and Kayla have so many thoughts running through their minds. The bag could belong to Derek's drug habit, says Elena. Mariah thinks Derek is hiding something much bigger involving Darrius Rivers; he hung up the phone quickly when Mariah called Derek. Kayla, Elena, and Aiden suspect Darrius and Derek could be connected, but none know what it is. Aiden said he would dig deeper and return to that place in the dark alleyway. Elena warns Aiden to be careful and not to venture out alone. Kayla suggested bringing Jalen with him. So Aiden decided to take Jalen on the next outing.

CHAPTER 10

The next day comes, and Aiden meets up with Jalen again at a secret location. Jalen gets in Aiden's car, and they drive to the area where Derek is looking for something. They decided to go inside today, so Aiden entered the dark and muggy. Room. They both use a flashlight on their phones, and then as they are walking through the area, Jalen steps on something. It was something wet. So as Jalen was walking through the darkness, both Aiden and Jalen turned around and saw a girl, a skinny, frail girl, on the floor, disoriented and not talking. She quivers as Jalen turns around; she is tied to a chair. Then they heard the door slam; Aiden and Jalen booted out of there so fast they left skid marks on the floor.

When they got to the car, Jalen wanted to go to the cops. All they found was a girl beaten up and tied to a chair. Aiden tried to calm down Jalen, but Jalen couldn't get the image of the girl out of his head. She was very skinny, with clothes ripped and a bloody lip with a black eye. She looked beat up. Jalen wanted to take this information to the cops, but Aiden disagreed; he thinks the cops won't do anything without hard-core evidence. Jalen thought this was too much and remembered Kayla telling him that her friend is a 911 dispatcher, so Aiden and Jalen decided to contact Tori. Firstly they had to get her private number from Kayla. So Jalen calls up Kayla and gets her phone number.

Jalen makes the call and explains the situation to Tori. She told Jalen she would look into it, but I don't think there isn't much Tori could do because she's only a dispatcher. But Jalen thought Tori could inform detectives of the girl's location before Derek returned. Tori said she would try but isn't making any promises. Tori even mentioned that if they wanted, Aiden and Jalen could contact the police in Port Sunfield if they wished. Aiden and Jalen figured this situation would be too much and got there before Derek returned. Aiden calls up Elena and explains that this job is getting way too disturbing. Jalen and Aiden seeing the girl tied up like that freaked them out. The girls felt terrible for the boys and almost put them in danger. Elena warned Aiden to stay away from Derek and the spooky house. It was way too risky. Now they all know Derek Charlise is hiding something. Mariah wants to find out what it is, though.

The next day, Mariah, Kayla, and Elena walk to the nearest Library. There, they meet up with Gretchen Wellsford. Gretchen Wellsford has been in this town for many years, and she never thought such things could happen in such a quiet town. When she found out the girls were trying to solve a mystery in the city, Gretchen offered to show the girls something. She strolled over to the other side of the hall, and she picked up a book. Gretchen opened the book and showed the girls a picture. The pictures were of young ladies from ages fifteen to seventeen. Gretchen explained that the book was in their memory of the missing girls, and the girls thought this book looked uncomfortable. The girls felt dreadful about the whole situation. They kept looking at the picture of one of the girls and felt so sad. Girls fourteen and over go missing, and people in town don't know this is happening. Elena decides to snap a picture of the images and send it to Aiden. To see if Aiden can recognize anyone in those missing female pictures. Back in Port Sunfield, Aiden gets a text message from Elena. He opened the text message and it showed the photos of the missing ladies.

Elena tells Aiden to look at the pictures and see if there's anyone they recognize in the picture. That's when Aiden saw the image of this young girl with long black hair and brown eyes. He knew the moment he saw her, and it was the girl he and Jalen saw at the back of the spooky house. Aiden texts Elena back and tells her this information. Elena wondered why Jalen and Aiden didn't save the girl. The boys explained they found her tied to a chair, and Derek showed up, so they couldn't get the girl out in time. However, they have a plan for later to go back to the house and see if she is there. They're just hoping the girl is still there and not moved. Elena and the girls thought the plan was risky. Aiden and Jalen never told the girls much information about the girl in the house because they had never given her any names. The girl's name was unknown, and they could not save her in time.

Elena suggested they get a cop to check it out, and Mariah thinks getting a cop involved now wouldn't do as much. She thinks this way because the cops will search the place, but there isn't much they can do without evidence of a struggle. So then, the girls decided to keep this to themselves with the help of Gretchen Wellsford. Now back in Port Sunfield, Aiden wakes up from a horrifying dream. He sees the girl in the house in his dreams. I guess seeing the girl like that did a number on him. As Aiden wakes up from the nightmare, he gets a call from Jalen. Jalen told Aiden he would meet up with Jasper when the hell broke loose.

Derek showed up instead with a group of men and jumped Jalen. Derek asked questions interrogating him for hours about what he saw back at that house. Derek knows Aiden and Jalen were following him because two of Derek's friends saw Aiden and Jalen walk into that house. The two guys reported back to Derek and found out their description. Aiden then asked how they let Jalen go. Derek initially refused to let Jalen go because he and the others wanted to beat him even more and then tie him up. Derek knew Jalen had seen something that deserved to be incriminated. That would be the girl who was at the spooky house. To protect himself, Derek decided to kidnap Jalen and beat him up to keep the cops from finding out what happened. Derek and his gang left Jalen tied up with no way to escape after leaving him for a short period. After that, Jalen managed to escape and found the bag. Jalen managed to free himself by using the pocket knife in his back pants and cutting the ropes. He searched the rooms but could not locate the missing girl. Derek and his gang must have moved her. Therefore, Jalen was able to get away before Derek saw him. Since Derek didn't see Jalen before he fled, Jalen waited for his gang to leave before running. Jalen saw one of Derek's men throwing the bag in the trash junk and then getting into a car and going. When they left, Jalen ran outside the house and ran around the house; then, he walked up to the trash, picked up a garbage bag, and started running. After Jalen explained everything, Aiden didn't seem surprised, but he was happy he got the sack last.

Weird how everything broke loose. After Jalen explained what had happened to him, Jalen texted Kayla; the girls were shocked by Derek. Everyone knew Derek was a criminal. Just look at the past, when he pushed Mariah, his ex-wife, down the stairs. So it wasn't unexpected to Mariah that Derek and his guys beat up Jalen. The good news is that Jalen wasn't too beat up. He got some minor cuts and bruises from the ropes, and he will recover. In other information, as the girls got off the phone with Jalen, the girls carried on with their day; they left the Library and decided to go to a coffee shop for a lovely afternoon. The most significant thing is the bag that Jalen found. When Jalen and Aiden returned home, they opened the bag to see various girls' devices, gadgets, ropes, IDs, and cell phones. Jalen was astonished as Aiden was freaked out more than ever. Jalen calls Kayla, explains what they found, and asks Kayla, Mariah, and Elena to keep the information.

CHAPTER 11

It is the afternoon in Craven Heights. Elena, Kayla and Mariah have made it to the coffee shop. Elena told the girls to find a place to sit. Elena went up to the cash register and ordered lattes for the three. The girls started drinking the latte and chit-chatted some more about the mystery in town. Kayla will continue to investigate the city with the help of her friends. After the chit-chat, the ladies decided to get out of the coffee shop and get more information on Darrius Rivers. Kayla will continue to investigate the city with the help of her friends. Kayla will continue to explore the city with the help of her friends.

The girls decided to walk to the graveyard because they thought Darrius might be there again. It looked like their guess was correct because Darrius was there again; he kept looking at a picture on a gravestone. Mariah decided to walk up to him and ask about the image. Darrius looked at Mariah and thought to himself; there she goes again. Darrius opened up to Mariah; he mentioned that the girl's picture on the stone was his wife, Mella Harris Rivers. She died a couple of years ago, and Darrius comes to the graveyard to pay his respects. He misses her every day. He described her to be gentle, shy and sweet. Darrius continued to ask what brought Mariah here to the cemetery. Mariah told him, I was looking for you. Darrius was confused. Mariah mentioned how much he resembled her ex-husband; she asked Darrius again if he had any connection to Derek Charlise. Darrius looked nervous but then said he did not know Derek Charlise.

Mariah even mentioned that now is the time for anything he'd like to tell. Mariah even mentioned she knew about his past life as a criminal. Darrius says he is not a criminal; he did things in his past, like mischievous thefts. The article was accurate, but he learned from his mistakes after getting out of jail. Despite this, the community still views him as a felon. Darrius got so nervous and rambling on then eventually confessed that he is Derek's eldest half-brother and was sent to Craven Heights by Derek to watch Mariah, more specifically, the gallery. Mariah looked up at Darrius, wide-eyed, and thought she knew it! She knew Derek was planning to start trouble. There is no doubt that Mariah should have known this beforehand, but she still wanted to believe in Derek's goodness. Darrius proceeded to mention more information regarding Derek. He could not stop rambling on. Darrius told Mariah that Derek was planning something very significant. He wanted Mariah to be careful. He is working for criminals and is involved in a big scheme. Mariah found this information to be startling and appalling. So she ended the conversation with Darrius and wandered over to Elena and Kayla. Mariah explained the whole thing to them. Elena and Kayla were shocked that this was happening. Mariah even understood why Darrius looked like Derek because they were half-brothers. Mariah strolled up to Darrius and wondered if Derek was a counterpart or something. It all made sense now. Darrius laughed. The girls decided to leave the graveyard and said bye to Darrius. Darrius will leave town before Derek discovers that his ex-wife found out about his plan.

When the girls left the graveyard and went back into the business, Elena and Mariah returned to the gallery, and Kayla returned to her internship. The next couple of hours came; Kayla wrote away at Morgan's wonders. Elena and Mariah were busy at the gallery. Mariah put Elena to work. Sometimes Elena regrets not going to college because she could have done much more than be an art assistant. Though Elena does not hate her job as an art assistant, she is grateful she got a job. After cleaning up the boxes in the backroom, Elena couldn't help but think about the lost girl and the secretive bag that Aiden and Jalen found. She brought this thought up to Mariah. As soon as she mentioned it to Mariah, she too couldn't help but think about it. So Elena and Mariah finished up at the gallery, closed the shop and went back to their flat. Elena and Mariah took a shortcut to their flat. As they walked through the dark alleyway, they kept looking back, thinking about a town that was once good, not turned empty and grey. They go a few blocks, and they make it to their building. Elena and Mariah enter through the lobby, walk down the hall, and into the small elevator. Mariah presses the floor button, and the elevator goes up. They walk out of the elevator, down the aisle and make it to their door. They make it inside their flat, safe and sound.

The girls change into comfy nightwear and sit on the sofa. Just then, Elena remembered to call Aiden. So she gives Aiden a call and asks him about Jalen and how he is doing. She even warns Aiden to be careful while investigating. Aiden agrees with Elena. They continue to talk for the rest of the night. Mariah was in her room researching what Derek could be hiding. All Darrius told her was that Derek was planning something big with criminals. And that he does not want Mariah to find out. Derek wants Mariah to stay out of it, so he sends his eldest brother to fool Mariah. Yet, Mariah isn't falling for Derek's tricks. Whatever he is hiding, she is bound to find out with her friends. The night turned young. Mariah decided to close her laptop and headed to sleep. As for Elena, she ended the call.

Meanwhile, Kayla walks out of the Morgan Wonders office, gets on the local bus 52, and heads to her apartment. When she gets to the apartment, she takes her shoes and jacket off and runs into the washroom for a bath. After a bath, Kayla ventures to the kitchen for a snack. Then she strolls to the sofa, sits there and calls Mariah, but Mariah isn't picking up because she is sleeping. Mariah then texted Elena, and Elena didn't respond; Elena must have fallen asleep. So, she ends up calling her boyfriend Jalen, she checks upon him, and they talk for hours. As they were talking, Kayla told Jalen of the plan of sneaking into the

Mayor's office. Kayla was the only one who thought the Mayor was hiding something. She always thought the mayor was off when she stared at him on TV. She does not know why, but she had a terrible feeling when he talked about the missing girls. As Kayla is rambling on, Jalen makes a snoring noise. Kayla screams at Jalen to wake up. Jalen laughs; Kayla wants Jalen to get serious. Jalen apologized and said he would do better. He even mentioned getting struck by one of Derek's friends.

Kayla thought, why would Jalen put himself in that kind of danger? However, she remembered what a sweet soul Jalen was. The two continued talking till we hours. The call ended on its own.

The following day came, and Mariah woke up and walked to the kitchen. There she saw Elena already up and making breakfast. Mariah was wondering why Elena was up so early. Elena is never an early bird. I guess this morning was different for Elena. Elena ran up to Mariah and hugged her. These two have become such great friends. However, they can't forget that Kayla was one of their best friends. Too bad she can't get in on the hug this time. Elena grabbed her phone and opened Facebook, and it said she got a friend request from Aiden, so Elena told Mariah what she should do. I mean, that's the dummies' question. Mariah told her to accept Aiden, and Elena had received Aiden's friend request. That morning was excellent. Back at Kayla and Tori's apartment, Kayla just got up, made some coffee and sat on the sofa. Then she remembers that Tori left for work in the morning; she wanted to catch her before Tori left because she wanted

Tori to research the lost girl. So Kayla sends her a quick text. Tori responds instantly and tells her she will try her best to find information on her. But she didn't promise anything because she had other work to do.

Mariah also thought about the situation and talked to the girls before going to the police station the next day. She wanted to report what Darrius said to them. Eventually, the next day arrives, and Mariah, Elena, and Kayla make their way to the police station by bus. After arriving there, the girls walked to the front desk and spoke with a police officer about Darrius Rivers and Derek Charilise's plan. During the girls' hour at the police station talking with the detective responsible for the missing person case, he told the girls they would consider this. The girls then went about their day as they always do. Elena ordered a latté for everyone at the cash register. The girls drank the latte and talked about the mystery in town. Kayla and her friends will continue to investigate the city together.

Aiden and Jalen put aside the mystery of Derek and Darrius due to heavy school and work at the time. Now that he had returned to Port Sunfield, Jalen had finished his assignments. Aiden was also finishing up his previous studies. A few weeks had passed since Jalen's leg had healed up; he decided to visit Kayla. Jalen buys a two-way ticket and hops on the nearest travel bus to Craven Heights. After several hours, he makes it to Craven Heights. He hops off the bus, grabs his luggage, and hails a taxi to Kayla's apartment. After several hours, he makes it to Craven Heights. Kayla is at home cooking dinner until she hears a knock at the door, and as soon as she opens it, she sees Jalen. She jumps into his arms and hugs him. Jalen walks inside and greets Tori. It looked like Jalen Archwood was in town, and Elena and Mariah didn't know yet. So Kayla calls Elena and Mariah, and they come to visit Jalen. Everyone was together, besides Aiden. Aiden had some work to do, so he couldn't make it on the trip. But he will visit again soon. But the most important thing is solving the mystery. So that is another reason why Jalen is in town. It has been many weeks since the crew, Jalen, Mariah, Elena, and Kayla, discovered the lost girl from the spooky house likely had been moved somewhere else. When Jalen was locked up in the place, he searched every room except the basement. As per their initial guess, the lost girl is still inside the house, and the crew believes Derek was trying to confuse Jalen into thinking that the missing girl had been moved; however, she is still inside the house. With all this new information, the girls thought talking to Gretchen Wellsford may help with all this further information.

They all make it to Gretchen's house, and she greets the crew. She invites them in and makes them tea and cookies. They get right into business. I guess Gretchen knew why they were there. So she opened up a can of beans. She talked about the lost girl, the secret bag, Kayla's idea of the Mayor and the mysterious look of Derek's eldest half-brother Darrius. Gretchen gave the team some articles about the missing girls to see if this could be any information. She mentioned she had read the report of Darrius Rivers, but she never expected him to be related to one of Mariah's ex-husbands. Gretchen wanted to know how Mariah was doing hearing all of this. Mariah explained that she was okay; she would find out what Derek was doing. Gretchen said she would help with anything.

CHAPTER 12

Eight months from now. It has been a long since these girls have worked on this missing person case. It's April 2021; Kayla is finishing her internship at Morgan Wonders. She walks over to her boss to give her one last story. Even though Kayla's internship is finishing up, she won't stop writing; she will continue to write from home until she gets a new job. Back at the Gallery, Mariah and Elena are selling many paintings. Mariah thought giving Elena a job there was incredible because Elena has excellent working skills.

Now at Port Sunfield, it's April, the time for college students to be out of school. Jalen and Aiden are finishing up their last semester of engineering studies. Jalen is recovered and wants to find out what Derek is doing. Kayla thought that was a bad idea because Derek warned him to stay away. But the boys weren't giving up just yet. Aiden thought of a plan with Jalen. Both Aiden and Jalen will go to Derek's loft when he is not there and have a look around for any clues. Elena calls Aiden and tells them to be careful and stay there very long. The girls were definitely on a high edge, and they thought the boys would get caught.

Just then, Elena thought of a previous plan.

While the boys were keeping tabs on Derek, the girls would sneak into the Mayor's office at night.

Kayla thought Elena and Mariah were out of their minds. But Kayla just knew when she talked with the Mayor that he must know something they don't know. Mariah and Elena eventually got on board with this. Tonight the girls were going to sneak into the Mayor's office to find some traces. With that happening, Gretchen dropped her granddaughter, Layla, at school and then drove herself to the town library for work. On her way to work, she spots Mariah and Elena heading to the gallery that morning. The town is small, and everyone knows each other. But not everyone knows everything. Gretchen was wondering what the girls were doing. She thought to herself that she would call Elena after work. So the day went on, and the girls were finishing up work that day. Mariah and Elena close the shop and head to their loft. Kayla cleaned up her writing desk and left the office. While this was happening, Jalen and Aiden were getting ready to go to Derek's apartment. So the girls call Jalen and Aiden and let them know their plan to sneak into the Mayor's office. The boys thought they were crazy but thought this town needed some help, so they agreed.

They already have Tori working from the inside as a dispatcher to help the gang out with information coming into the dispatch. Mariah, Elena, Kayla, and the boys Jalen and Aiden could have taken this plan to the cops, but as Tori said, the cops wouldn't do much of anything without evidence. But, they all talked about it and decided not to go to the cops again.

Tori receives many calls from women in trouble, so she saves the recordings and shares them with the girls. Currently, it is 10:00 pm in Craven Heights, and everyone is fast asleep. The girls dressed in black drive over to Mayor Kaiser's office. In search of a back door, the girls utilize a hairpin to open it. After seeing the security camera in front of the back door, Kayla smashed it to prevent the camera from recording the girls. After doing so, they all found a way inside. Each girl goes inside individually. They stroll through the dark, empty hallway. They turned into coroners and then found the mayor's office upon entering. As the girls pass a shadowy figure, they freeze in their tracks.

The girls never felt so scared. Meanwhile, back in Port Sunfield, Aiden and Jalen are getting ready to go to Derek's loft.

Afterward, they get the car and drive to Derek's place. They saw Jasper Charlise, Derek's other and younger brother, coming out of the building when they arrived. Jalen noticed this and wondered where Derek was, and Aiden told him he could still be inside. So they held back for a while and regrouped. They waited hours upon hours to see if Derek would leave the building. Then just as they were about to give up, Jalen and Aiden spotted Derek leaving the building. They waited for Derek to get in his car and leave before entering. So when the coast was clear, both Aiden and Jalen made their way to the building. The building is high alert security, so Aiden and Jalen were cautious about entering the building. Dressed as police officers, the men walked to the entrance of the building and informed the security guard they were cops. They had a search warrant for one of the tenants. Security didn't suspect anything; he just rang the beep to let them in. So that they did, Aiden and Jalen got inside and took the elevator to the fifteenth floor. Aiden and Jalen got a bobby pin and unlocked Derek's apartment. They make their way inside and close the door behind them. Jalen told Aiden to look on one side while Jalen looked. Jalen was a bit confused about what he was trying to find. After hours of exploring the place, Aiden and Jalen found a box with a key, So the guys thought that was interesting and took it. Jalen and Aiden finished up what they were doing, grabbed the box, and left.

After they fled the scene, the boys hopped in their car, got in, and drove away. On the way home, Jalen and Aiden accidentally called Elena on the phone, and her phone started ringing so loudly. Kayla and Mariah told her to turn it off before anyone heard it. However, it was too late. Just as they were getting ready to run for office, the girls found a picture on the Mayor's desk and grabbed it as they were sorting through papers. The Mayor's security eventually caught the girls. Police were called, and the girls were taken to the police station in town. The cops also took the mysterious picture. Back in Sunsfield, the boys have no idea where the girls are. Their plan didn't work. As the girls were being taken to the station, Detective Finley Jones interrogated them one by one. Elena was the first to be questioned, followed by Mariah, then Kayla. The girls made no statements. Cops wanted to know why the girls broke into the mayor's office. They contemplated telling them but didn't say anything.

They asked for a phone call. So Elena calls Gretchen Wellsford and tells them what happened. Gretchen is shocked to hear this and sad that this terrible thing happened to them. She drives to the girls.

Meanwhile, Jalen and Aiden tried to get into the box; they even had a key. But they decided to wait till they told the girls. So, Aiden calls up Mariah and tells her about what they found in Derek's apartment. Then Mariah informs Jalen and Aiden that they just got out of prison. While it may seem easy to get out of jail, this case was handled by Gretchen, who was able to bail out the girls.

Aiden and Jalen wanted to know if the girls needed any help because they were appalled. The girls said no. They got lucky because Ms. Gretchen bailed them out. It was a very long night, and the girls told Aiden and Jalen to keep the box. They agreed on their plan. Gretchen then dropped the girls home.

It's a new day in Craven Heights. After the girls had a crazy night in jail, they decided to find out what was in the box. Elena calls Aiden, and he sends her a picture of the box. The only problem now is opening the package. Elena, Mariah, and Kayla were very curious to see what was in the box. The box belonged to Derek, so they wanted to know what Derek was keeping in that box. Afterward, Aiden told the girls they would figure out how to open it. So after a few minutes, Jalen sharpened the key, pressed into the box's hole, and opened it.

There inside lay pictures of plenty of girls. The photos showed girls tied up, posing, and looking miserable. The boys were surprised to see all of these pictures of girls tied up like animals. The boys started connecting the photos to the IDs they found in the bag the previous day. The girls were disturbed by these pictures of innocent girls. On the other end of the line, Mariah grabbed the phone from Elena and kept looking at the pictures. She thought she had known Derek all his life, but she didn't know much about him. Mariah was married for two years to Derek. She knew Derek had a past in those two years, but she never understood it.

Elena even asked Mariah whether there was anything suspicious about Derek when they were married. Mariah explained to the girls that Derek used to keep to himself, and he always hid his phone. Mariah just thought he was cheating, which he was. However, it turns out that there was more to that. Elena ended the call and tried to comfort Mariah. It must have come as a shock to her. Mariah understands now that Derek wasn't who she thought he was.

After a while, Aiden had a theory and believed Derek had found his long-lost half-brother Darrius Rivers and contacted him. Then, he came up with a plan for Darrius Rivers to follow Mariah and her friends to track and distract them from the real thing. Yet, the team is not sure what they exactly found. They had seen the lost girl, the box with pictures of innocent girls, the bag with IDs and devices, and Derek working with someone. The only thing missing is that the team doesn't know who that someone is. The girls thought there was a connection between Derek and the lost girls. The question still plays; the girls wanted answers. So the only place to go for answers is the library. So off they went; Elena texted Aiden back and ended the conversation. The following day, the ladies went to the library where Gretchen Wellsford works. She tells them to get inside quickly. Gretchen doesn't want the girls to end up back in jail. She even asked them what they were doing in the Mayor's office. The girls explained they wanted to know if the mayor had anything to do with the missing girls.

Gretchen giggled; she thought the girls thinking Mayor Kaiser was responsible for the missing girls was absurd.

Gretchen said she would help with anything, but at the same time, she thought about things and warned the girls to stop digging into something they couldn't handle. The girls thought Gretchen was a touch mean, but it was true. Gretchen was only trying to protect them. She did not want the girls to become missing like the other girls.

So the girls talked it over with Gretchen and decided to leave the mystery to the boys until they figured out what to do. Meanwhile, Jalen and Aiden were on a hot trail. They found Derek's box, and the mysterious bag and understand that Darrius and Derek are related, but nobody knows yet if there is a connection between Derek and the missing girls. That's when Kayla called Jalen. She told him about the picture they found in Mayor Kaiser's office, and that girl could be Gretchen's long-lost daughter because she resembles Gretchen. Jalen asked Kayla to get the image from the cop's office. So Kayla decided to sneak over to the police station.

That day, Elena distracts the cops while Kayla sneaks in through the back. She entered detective Finley Jones's room and searched everywhere for the picture. Elena texts Kayla to hurry up. So Kayla found one last place to explore; it was the desk behind the table. She opened it, and there was the picture. She grabbed it and hit the road so fast, leaving Elena behind. Elena eventually caught up with her. She was out of breath from all the running. They got in their cars, looked at the picture, and sent it to Gretchen. Two seconds later, Gretchen confirmed that the image they found was Gretchen's long-lost daughter. Who knows where she could be now?

CHAPTER 13

Port Sunfield, lovely morning it is. Children and parents are running around getting things done for today. Schools closed, and parents returned to work. The town seemed alone and quiet. Nobody in the city suspected anything was going to happen.

Then suddenly, a man walking down the street gets struck by a vehicle. The man behind the wheel was none other than Derek Charlise. He wasn't looking at where he was heading, and he was running from something or someone. Of course, Derek would be the one who runs over someone.

Let's take a look back before the accident happened. Now, before the accident, Derek had a meeting at his job. He wakes up beside Clare, showers and changes his clothes. He then heads out. Derek hops in his car and drives to work that morning. He enters the building and meets with the board of trustees. After the meeting and hours of work later, Derek makes his way to his car, hops in, turns on the vehicle, and calls Clare. He and Clare talk for about five minutes. Derek then drives to this location outside of downtown Port Sunfield. He parked the car in the driveway and got out. As Derek gets out, two men come out of the house. They greet Derek, and he walks into the house. Derek passes by the house entrance and makes his way up the stairs. He walks up the stairs, turns right, then left, and enters this room. There you have a man sitting behind a chair. You can't see his face, but you can hear his voice. He is wearing a mask. The man asks Derek for the stuff. Derek hands over something. But it wasn't what the man wanted. The mystery man tells his bodyguards to escort Derek out.

Derek walks out of the room. He descends the stairs and runs to his car. Derek looked a bit freaked out and drove out of there really fast. He ran some red lights too. Derek exceeded the speed limit and hit a random man. Time rushes for Derek as he hits the poor guy. Derek comes out of his car for a second, and then people in the street are yelling at Derek.

Derek hated the commotion, so he returned to his vehicle and fled the scene. Just then, cops and an ambulance come to the location and take the guy to the hospital. The man looked to be in his late fifties. Cops wanted the description of the hit and run. So some people near the scene started giving descriptions of Derek. Derek was on the radar of the police. The mystery man back at the house was getting shipments ready at home, and he walked out of the room with scary-looking big men. One of the men was an Asian-looking guy. The man that Derek wanted to see. Just then, the mystery man walks down the stairs, turns left and then right. He opens the basement door and makes his way down the stairs. There we see a young girl about the age of sixteen tied up. A man walks toward her and tells her to get up. She does what he says. She has a terrified look in her eyes.

The girl looks up at the guy and spits in his face. The big mystery man slaps her and tells his men to do whatever they want with her. All you could hear were cries in the room; more girls were down there. The mystery man walks out of the room like nothing is down there. He goes on about his day; the door to the basement gets locked with a code.

Meanwhile, Derek Charlise is on the loose. Police want him for a hit and run. And quite possibly illegal drugs. News of Derek's desire for an arrest spread fast across town, especially in Craven Heights. Elena and Mariah were at home relaxing when the news came on and a sketch of Derek appeared on TV. Mariah spits out her cereal. Elena was also startled. Kayla was organizing some clothes when she saw the illustration of Derek. She called Elena and Mariah. They already knew, so it wasn't a surprise. Back in Sunfield, Derek is on the run. He ran so far and had nowhere else to turn.

Derek then finds a gas station and a payphone and calls his eldest half-brother Darrius Rivers. He wanted an update on Mariah's whereabouts. Darrius mentioned that he did not care anymore; he had already told Mariah what was up. So Derek got so angry, told him you're going to pay and disconnected the phone. Then after a couple of seconds, Derek thought of another person that could help him out: his other brother Jasper. But, it turned out that

Jasper couldn't help him out. He doesn't want to associate with his big brother, so he hangs up the phone. So Derek had no one left except for Jalen. During the month of December 2020, he beat up Jalen because he thought he could force him to help him. Back in Port Sunfield, Jalen is in his loft when he gets a call from Kayla warning him about Derek being on the loose. So as Jalen was talking to Kayla, Jalen got a knock at the door and told Kayla to hold on. He would answer the door, so he did, and Derek pointed a gun at Jalen. Jalen froze in his tracks and told Kayla he would call her back.

Kayla didn't like the tone in Jalen's voice. She knew something was wrong. Kayla grabs her keys, says bye to Tori, and sets off on her way to Mariah and Elena's house. When she gets there, she frantically knocks on the door. Elena opens it, hugs her, and Kayla spills everything. She tells them Jalen must be in trouble. Mariah thought it was time to call the cops now. Kayla agreed, except for Elena. Elena wanted Aiden to check on Jalen. But things have become too risky. Having made his way back to Jalen's place, Derek is standing over Jalen, holding a gun to his forehead. Derek sure looked like he had lost his mind. He tells Jalen to sit on the chair. Derek ties Jalen up. Jalen mentions to Derek that he's a scumbag and is nothing like Darrius Rivers. He also says that Derek doesn't care about his family, like his other brother Jasper and his late sister-in-law Mella. Derek rolled his eyes and bad-mouthed Jalen. However, Jalen wasn't planning to give any information to Derek. He knew he was a psychopath. So Jalen kept his mouth shut. Derek took Jalen's credit cards and bank cards and tied him tightly to the chair. He duck-taped Jalen's mouth and then fled the scene. The main reason why Derek fled the scene was that he was a wanted criminal and did not have the time and energy to carry out a kidnapping plot, so his primary concern was reaching his boss.

Aiden arrives at Jalen's apartment two hours later and is outraged to see Jalen bound up and duct-taped. He unties Jalen and takes the duct off. Aiden knew it was Derek that tied Jalen up. So he didn't ask too many questions. They just had to follow after him. First, they called Kayla and the girls to inform them what Derek had done. The girls were horrified, especially Kayla. Jalen reassures Kayla that he's fine, just a bit shaken up. He explained to Kayla that Derek had stolen his bank cards and visa. Derek was making a run for it and could make a run to where his ex-wife Mariah was. So Jalen warns the girls that Derek might be coming to town. She then decides to inform Tori what's happening. She agrees to call the police. It's getting too risky now, and everyone's lives might be in danger.

Meanwhile, in Port Sunfield, the mystery man has men watching the house. While that is happening, Derek is still on the run. The girls are at home watching the news. Kayla and Tori head to Mariah and Elena's house, where they call the cops. Mariah explains to the cops what could be happening. The girls filled in everything about Derek and his eldest half-brother that told him to stalk Mariah. The cops thought what she was saying didn't make sense; however, the cops wanted to trust her.

The truth is coming to light, Derek is a vicious criminal. He ran over an innocent person and fled. Now Derek is a fugitive. The cops wanted to catch Derek and whoever he was working with to put them behind bars. Mariah thought she could trick Derek into confessing.

Mariah is his ex-wife, and he listens to her and what she has to say. There is no talk between the girls and the cops at the moment. So Mariah and the girls hatch a plan to catch Derek and the mystery man behind the mask.

The following day, Elena, Kayla, and Mariah arrive in Sunfield. It is crazy how fast time flies. But they're only in this town to catch Derek and finally put him behind bars where he belongs. The next thing you know, Mariah gets a call from an unknown number. It turns out it's Clare Willow. Derek's new wife. Mariah wondered why Clare was calling. She said she saw the news and wanted to end things with Derek because he had lost his mind. She told Clare to shut up and hung up as if Mariah cared. Elena laughed about Clare; Mariah explained that Clare was clueless about Derek. Elena was eager to resolve the matter. Consequently, Elena, Mariah, and Kayla drove to Aiden's place.

Jalen and Aiden were inside researching. Jalen opens the door, and Kayla hugs him. The girls get settled in for a bit and then get to their plan. Mariah was assigned to take the baton while Kayla and Elena were lookouts. Aiden was assigned to work with Jalen. However, Aiden thought about the house Derek was coming in and out of many months ago. So far, nobody knows where Derek is. Before they did the plan, Mariah decided to call Derek to find out what he was doing. So she calls Derek, and Derek picks up the phone. Mariah tells Derek to come clean and tell her who his boss is. Derek rambled on irrationally and proceeded to threaten her and her friends. Aiden and Jalen decide to drive to the house with the girls. The plan was in motion. Men were surrounding the house, back and front.

Aiden and Elena walk around the back of the house. Elena noticed that it was a highly secure house with cameras. She first devises a plan to distract the man. Elena dresses up as a bodyguard and pretends to be one of them. Walking into the house, she marches around the back of the room. Her eye catches the sight of a bodyguard standing guard at the back entrance. As she walks up to him pretending to report something, she kicks him in the face, knocking the gun from his hands, and then she grabs the gun. There was an outburst of violence in the air. At the same time, Elena smashes one of the security cameras and then unlocks the back door for Aiden to walk inside the house.

Kayla, Mariah, and Jalen were at the front of the house while this was going on. Kayla, Mariah, and Jalen planned to distract the men in front of the house. Two men were guarding the front entrance, and then Jalen got behind the wheel of his car and slammed into the men and the place.

The door breaks into pieces. All you hear are gunshots. Mariah, Kayla, and Jalen get inside the house. Inside they find the team, Elena and Aiden. The group decides to split up. Outside the house, two men are lying on the ground, unconscious. Meanwhile, Derek Charlise was still on the run. He got a call from an unknown number, and it was the mystery man. The mystery man asked him to meet him at the house. Derek refused. Derek assumed it was a trap. The mystery man threatened Derek, telling him that my guys would find and kill his ex-wife, Mariah if he didn't show up. As cold-blooded as Derek was, he didn't give a damn. During that exchange, the mystery man asked Derek how Clare was doing. He told Derek he saw men surrounding Clare's apartment. He had to obey what the man was telling him for Clare's sake. Derek then drove to the house to meet the mystery man.

Meanwhile, inside the house, the girls split up with the guys. Elena, Kayla, and Mariah turn left, and Jalen and Aiden turn right. They try to cover as much of the house as possible. Many of the men are knocked out in front of the house. After fifteen minutes, Elena finds a locked door that she cannot open. It is the basement. The door would not budge even though she tried to open it. You have to put your thumbprint on it to unlock it. It took the girls and guys a while to figure out you could use one of the men's thumbs to open the door. In this case, one of the girls, Elena, and one of the guys, Aiden, grabbed one of the unconscious men's bodies and moved it toward the basement door. Elena then suggested that Aiden put the thumb of the guy on the door and that they plant it there. So that is what Aiden did precisely. Within seconds, the door began to unlock and open. Elena was one of the girls to go down the stairs. She saw a young woman tied up as she walked down the stairs. Elena quickly takes out her phone and flips through her pictures. She looks at the picture, then at the girl. Elena then figures out that the female in the picture is one of the girls they found in that box. Then, she screamed for Aiden, Jalen, and Kayla to hurry down to the basement. Aiden and Jalen walk in first, then Kayla walks in. Mouth dropped on both sides. Elena quickly shows the photo of the girl to Kayla, Jalen, and Aiden. They all agree that this is the girl. The girl is tied to a wall wearing the same clothing she wore in that photo. Elena was the one to make the connection.

CHAPTER 14

The team is in the basement; they untie the girl and ask her name. She told them she was Destiny Araia. She is a twenty-two-year-old woman who is shy, delicate and kind. The woman was wearing jeans and a ripped shirt. Years ago, when she was eighteen years old, she was kidnapped by a group of men. The team was shocked and didn't believe they had found Gretchen's long-lost daughter. A group of men abducted girls to satisfy their disgusting selves. They enjoyed inflicting pain on others. They kidnapped Destiny for years; she was very thirsty and needed water. So they try to get her out of the basement and out of the house without being caught. It is believed that the men around the house are unconscious because when the car hit the car, they jumped out of the way and knocked themselves out.

So because of that, the team decides to make a run for it. Aiden steals one of the men's cars; Elena grabs the key from the man and gives it to Aiden. He starts the car. Destiny sat in the back seat with Elena while Kayla sat in front of Mariah. Jalen was in the passenger seat, and Aiden was driving. The team gets out of there and goes to the nearest hospital. Elena decides to call Gretchen with the good news that her daughter is alive. Elena calls Gretchen and explains the situation. Gretchen didn't believe her at first. She had to see if what Elena was saying was true with her own eyes. The team arrives at the hospital, and doctors and nurses take Destiny into a room. Elena and the crew sit in the waiting room and wait for Gretchen.

One hour later, Gretchen arrives. Elena runs up to her, she explains again, and the doctor talks to Gretchen about Destiny. Gretchen then asks Elena and the girls to watch over Layla while Gretchen goes and sees Destiny. The doctor takes Gretchen into the room to reunite with her long-lost daughter. Gretchen's eyes fill up with tears. Gretchen then gives Destiny the biggest hug ever. It has been several years since she last saw her daughter. The cops come to the hospital to ask Destiny some questions, but Mariah tells them off. It just wasn't the time to ask questions when Destiny was traumatized. A lot has happened in the last hour, but it wasn't quite over yet.

Aiden was searching through the list of missing girls, and he thinks since they found destiny there at the house, there could be more girls there locked up. So Elena says we have to go and check; Aiden said to leave it to the cops because the wicked men are probably swarming the house by now. The Mystery Man arrives home with his gang of muscular men. Few muscular men get killed for not doing their job and letting Destiny escape. The mystery man thought the girls and the guys knew too much and should kill them. Just then, at the hospital, Detective Finley

Jones thanks the girls for their effort and rescue and that the cops got it from here. The girls weren't giving up just yet. They wanted to go back to the house to see more girls there. Elena told Detective Finley that if cops show up at the house and barge in with an FBI squad, whoever is in the place will be killed. Detective Finley Jones is a forty-year-old man who is bossy and brave in the field. He tells the girls he thanks them for their help, but the cops handle the rest from here. Elena walks away from the detective and goes to Gretchen. Elena explains to Gretchen that she feels there are more missing girls. And if they don't act fast now, the girls will be moved and shipped somewhere else. Gretchen covers for them while the team returns home.

Twenty-four hours from now. Elena, Kayla, Mariah, Aiden, and Jalen figure out a plan for getting back into the house. They noticed last time; that the men wore cloaks. They stopped at Gretchen's home before they got to the house, where she had black robes. I guess Gretchen likes to wear weird clothes and the colour black. So they get their costumes on and disguise themselves as men. The team makes it to the house. First, Kayla and Mariah followed Elena. Aiden and Jalen are in the vehicle and are on the lookout. Aiden texts Elena immediately before she enters the house. Elena walks inside the house, and nobody suspects her. Then Mariah walks behind her, and then Kayla walks in. The girls made it inside. They follow the men in cloaks to this underground room where the mystery man appears. The girls are there witnessing this. The mystery man reveals himself to be Kaiser Beckett.

Kayla whispered she knew it, and she knew the Mayor was involved. Elena and Mariah thought it was Derek the whole time, but it wasn't. Derek worked as Kaiser's sidekick.

In her mind, Mariah wanted to cry. She was once married to Derek, and to find out that he was involved was a shocking revelation. She could never have imagined that Derek could have been involved in such an act of crime. Elena tried to calm Mariah down. With everything happening so fast, Mayor Kaiser brings out a few ladies who are all tied up. Just as that was happening, Elena's phone rang off. She forgot to turn on silent. Everyone stares at her, but Kaiser doesn't know who she is yet; he tells her to come forward. He reads the message Aiden sent to her and yanks off her mask. Mayor Kaiser had the evilest smile. It was a disaster; Kaiser tells his men to bring the two other ladies forward. Just as Kayla and Mariah were preparing to make a run for it, the men stopped them. Now their masks were revealed as well; There was a riot.

Kaiser said, looking at Kayla, and he remembered her when she had come to see him. Kayla wasn't trying to show him she was scared, so she spat in Kaiser's face. She was so enraged. Kaiser gives her a big slap across the face. Elena and Mariah scream at Kaiser not to touch her and how he won't get away with this. Just then, outside, Aiden and Jalen were watching what was happening. Aiden wanted to do something to prevent the girls from getting killed, so he called a detective - Finley Jones, a thirty-three-year-old, courageous, and proficient individual and explained a possible drug ring could be going on. Finley told the kids to stay out of it and was mad they disobeyed the law. He said he would get the police to the house immediately. While the cops were on the way, Kaiser told his men to send the girls to the basement. Elena, Kayla, and Mariah were confined with the rest of the missing ladies in another room.

They knew then that this was some drug ring. Kaiser continued to laugh in their faces; he thought he had won.

But think again. Derek tried to warn Kaiser that cops were on the way and had to get out of there. Kaiser told Derek to shut up. He even said that he would feed him to the cops. Kaiser mentioned that the cops wouldn't know he was responsible because Kaiser planned for Derek to take the fall. So Derek wouldn't let that happen, so he whipped out a knife and tried to stab Kaiser in the chest. Kaiser was too fast for him and took the knife and dropped it.

Kaiser got so ticked off, but Derek didn't care. Things were getting more complex. Aiden and Jalen were outside in the car waiting. One of Kaiser's men spots Aiden and Jalen and takes them forcibly inside. They drop them on the ground; Kaiser's minions laugh in their faces and think their master Kaiser will win. Kaiser walks upstairs and sees Jalen and Aiden and laughs at them. He ties up Jalen and Aiden. Back in the basement, the girls try to untie their hands so that they can escape. It was tough for them, and they wanted to run so badly.

Meanwhile, at the police station, detective Finley Jones and his men are fast approaching the house. They know Derek is in that house with the missing girls. So as they arrived, the FBI surrounded the building. The cops tell Derek to get out with his hands up. Kaiser tries to run for it; he runs down the hall through the living room. Then Derek trips him, so they begin to struggle. The cops can see the commotion from outside with their laser guns. The detective counted on three shots fired, hitting Kaiser in the back, and then Derek tried to make a run for it out the back door. They tried to aim at the criminals but couldn't figure out which one was who.

A cold night has fallen in the town of Port Sunfield; the police and FBI have surrounded the house. The detective, Finley Jones, walks into the house and proceeds to the living room, where he finds the mayor bleeding profusely on the floor. Derek is then trying to escape, and the detective finely shoots at him to stop him from running out the back door. He runs outside the house, but other cops catch him before escaping. Eventually, one of the cops tackled Derek down and took him into custody at the back of the house. Elena, Mariah and Kayla are still chained up inside the basement. Jalen and Aiden are in the living room tied up. Several police officers surround the entire property and head into the living room. Finley Jones walks over to Mayor Kaiser and checks to see if he is alive.

They confirmed that he was alive and transported him to the hospital as soon as they checked him. Cops untie Jalen and Aiden and take them to the ambulance. Then cops run down to the basement and find the girls tied up inside. They untie them and find other missing girls inside the house too. The cops were so stunned to see so many victims inside the basement. They take Mariah, Elena, and Kayla out first, and they get checked. At the same time, detective Finley Jones heads to the missing girls. The cops found four missing girls. The names of the lost girls were Elizabeth Meadows, Ariel Molley, Sky Marshall, and Jenny Noel. There were no deceased; the girls were alive. The truth about the mysterious town was coming to light. There was finally light at the end of the tunnel. The missing girls are going to ambulances and St John's Hospital. As for the gang, they also get sent to the hospital to get checked out.

A doctor examined Elena, Mariah, and Kayla at the hospital. The doctor looked at Jalen and Aiden because Kaiser had tied them down, so they were still in shock. The officers even brought Jalen his wallet and bank cards. They found everything on Derek. It looks like the team will have to stay in the hospital overnight. Detective Finley Jones wants to speak with the ladies during their hospital stay. He turns to Elena first, then to Mariah, and then Kayla. Jalen and Aiden get questioned as well.

I guess this was a standard procedure for police officers. Derek Charlise was sent to a downtown prison to await his trial upon his arrest. He is in custody at the prison centre. As for Mayor Kaiser Beckett, he has been transported to the nearest hospital, slated to undergo surgery on his left chest. Though the bullet missed his artery, he will survive. A police officer is watching the room of Mayor Kaiser Beckett. The breaking news reveals that the seven missing women are alive an hour later. Nobody is hurt. It was amazing to see how everyone in town was so happy and relieved that there was finally peace.

Mayor Kaiser is currently being charged with three kidnapping and drug trafficking counts. During Derek Charlise's trial, Derek Charlise confessed that he got mixed up with the wrong crowd and kidnapped women and sold them for millions of dollars.

Derek decides to plead guilty to the charges a few days later. Derek even admitted that he encouraged his half-brother to stalk his ex-wife to distract her from finding out about the missing girls. There are reports that Derek told authorities that he was introduced to Kaiser by a business associate who met him in Craven Heights. During the meeting, he became involved in the crime. Kaiser posed as a mayor to fool several people into thinking he was a kind and righteous man. However, that was not only the case; he fooled everyone, including the town of Craven

Heights. Before he became Mayor Kaiser, he was known as Kaiser Becket, the smuggler; nobody knew his real name because he was not from Craven Heights; he was from Port Sunfield. Therefore, when he became the Mayor of Craven Heights, he believed Kaiser had this power of authority and could get away with any crime he wanted.

After that, he met Derek and from then on, Derek unleashed Darrius Rivers on Kayla and her friends to confuse them. They began sending texts to the girls and making calls to them to scare them off. It turned out that Derek got the girl's number through Mariah's old cell phone that she used when the two of them were married. He found the number of her friend through Mariah's old cell phone. Plus, it turns out that Derek and Darrius are half-brothers. They come from the same mother, but they have different fathers.

CHAPTER 15

One week passes, and the ladies are back in Craven Heights; the boys are still in Port Sunfield. The trial for Derek Charlise and Mayor Kaiser started. It was a very busy long trial with a judge, prosecutor and defendant. The course went on for weeks among weeks. Finally, the jury came to a verdict, and Derek Charlise was found guilty of all counts of kidnapping and will have a sentence of 10 years without the possibility of parole. Mayor Kaiser gets life in prison without the possibility of parole. Kaiser will be transferred to a high state security prison because he broke the rule of the mayor code. News of Mayor Kaiser turned criminal was a shock to everyone. Craven Heights was mainly shocked because their Mayor played a heavy part in kidnapping the innocent girls.

Three weeks pass; it's a lovely afternoon in May, the birds are chirping, and the Children are playing outside. The town feels much at peace now that the mystery is solved. The ladies are going back to their lives in Craven Heights. They are ready to put this behind them. Gretchen Wellsford is thrilled about the ladies' effort to rescue the missing girls. Even though nobody believed them, they never gave up. Jill Asher is a thirty-five-year-old woman who is a lively, calm, and kind person. The woman is wearing a blouse and black dress pants. She awards the girls a medal for bravery and rescue at the city hall. A new Mayor will come to town, and this time, it will be someone citizens feel comfortable around. There is no Mayor for Craven Heights, but the city has to hope for a peaceful town.

Meanwhile, in Craven Heights, detective Finley Jones reunites the missing girls with their families. Families of the lost girls came to the hospital and ran up to them. They gave the biggest hugs and kisses. While the reunion was happening, the detective and Gretchen respected the citizens. That afternoon, the girls decided to stop by Gretchen's Wellsford house.

Gretchen reunited with her long-lost daughter five weeks ago, and they wanted to see how she was doing.

Destiny Araia was the first lady to escape the house of horrors. It was an homage to meet her and see how she adjusted to life outside a basement. The girls get in their car, arrive at Gretchen's place, and knock on the door. Then, Gretchen opens it and invites them in. Elena, Mariah, and Kayla sat down in the living room. Gretchen offers them some tea and cookies. Next thing you know, Destiny walks into the room. The ladies were so very amazed to see her walking and talking. Destiny missed her family, but most importantly, her daughter, whom she left when she was a baby. As the ladies listened to Destiny's story, they couldn't help but tear up. The ladies thought Destiny was a powerful girl to survive many years of torment in that cold, disgusting wet basement. Hearing her story made them want to open up about their struggles before coming to Craven Heights. Destiny explained what had happened to her before the story of her kidnapping. Whenever she walked to school, she noticed a young man staring at her as she walked by.

A few days later, the man looking at her grabbed her by the arm and threw her into the car. As soon as the ladies heard this, they started to cry. Afterward, the ladies talked about their lives with Destiny, and she was interested in becoming friends with the ladies.

One week has passed since the girls met up with destiny, and Craven Heights looks more beautiful and sunny than ever before. Suddenly, the city bursts into happiness, and Kayla wakes up and flings Tori off the bed. The two of them laughed. I would also like to point out that Kayla is preparing herself for a prestigious job interview. Kayla gets ready for a prestigious job. She finished her writing piece of the mystery in town at her last job for Morgan wonders. She recently started a new job at Vison Media centre as a content writer. Kayla was very excited about writing at her first job and wanted to turn her life into a story. This idea became her own, and she introduced it to her new boss, Kevin Tomas. Kevin is a twenty-five-year-old man who is bossy and arrogant. Although he is much older than Kayla, he is also charming when he wants to be. Kayla ignored the appearance and attitude that he possessed. Kayla just wanted to do her job professionally. Also, she has Jalen, so Kevin doesn't mean anything to Kayla. However, Jalen gets a bit jealous when he hears about Kayla's boss being a young man in his thirties. But Kayla tells Jalen not to be worried.

Meanwhile, at the Talen Gallery, Elena runs errands for Mariah. It is a busy day at the gallery. People were coming into the gallery looking to buy photos. Elena was cashing a few people out. Then the door opens again, and it's Destiny Araia, Gretchen's Daughter. Destiny walks in with her daughter Layla. Elena and Mariah were delighted to see Destiny again. Destiny apologizes for intruding. Elena and Mariah tell her it's okay; she's not intruding. Elena decides to give Destiny a tour of the place. Layla sits down with Mariah. It was all, in all, a lovely day. Back in Port Sunfield, Aiden and Jalen got summer jobs.

Jalen is a bartender, and Aiden is working as a sales advisor. The two commutes to work, come home, spend time together, and continue their business. It just so happens that back in Craven Heights, the fair took place. Parents and children around the city are excited to attend and have some fun, trying the rides, eating delicious food, and taking pictures.

Everything seemed to be changing around town. People around town are finally starting to get out more now that the criminal is behind bars. Kayla is enjoying her first job as a content writer, Mariah and Elena are showing destiny around, and Jalen and Aiden are enjoying their time back home in Sunfield.

Speaking of Derek, back in Port Sunfield, Derek Charlise is behind bars. He walks back and forth in his cell, and he even got beat up a few times by other inmates. As well as Mariah's gallery being taken away, that would never happen shortly. Former Mayor Kaiser is dragged out to Craven Heights, where he stays behind bars for life. A month passes, and there is no Mayor for Craven Heights yet. People around town are wondering when they will re-elect a mayor. It came as a shock when the citizens of Craven Heights found out their mayor was behind all of this crime. So, re-electing made everyone high on edge and nervous.

CHAPTER 16

It is a lovely day in Craven Heights. Everyone seemed happy and at peace. It was a Saturday, and the fair was in town. The ladies, Elena, Mariah, and Kayla, are getting ready to go out. They were on their way to the fair. They decided to meet Gretchen, Destiny, and Layla there. The news broke out that an election would start in the next month. Everyone at the fair was talking to one another. They spoke about what had happened months ago. Some people were moving past it. Others still were on the high edge. It came as a shock to see the mayor involved in a kidnapping. Nobody had a clue such things were happening around town. But now, everyone in the town wants to move past it.

Just a few weeks passed and it looked like something fun was going to happen in Craven Heights. It was known as the Town Fair. The fair was back in town. Families, children, and parents were all so excited to go there. The ladies, Elena, Mariah, and Kayla, were also happy to join. They met up with Gretchen Wellsford and her daughter Destiny, and, her granddaughter Layla. They were all attending together at the fair. A lot of things were happening during the fair. The fair brought the residents of Craven Heights together. The fair introduced tickets, puppet shows, rides, food, etc. Children of the town were running around having a good time. It looks like the city is finally moving past the nightmare. Elena, Mariah, and Kayla were going to Gretchen's house. The car pulls into the driveway; Elena gets out, walks to the door, and rings the doorbell. Gretchen answers the door, and little Layla runs up to Elena and hugs her.

She was so very excited about going to the town fair. She grabs Elena's hand, and they walk to the car.

Mariah and Kayla were in the car. They greet Layla with a hug as well. She has a bubbly personality, which makes her incredibly adorable. She is six years old.

Gretchen and Destiny take one car, and Elena, Mariah, and Kayla take another vehicle. They drive for thirty-five minutes and then arrive at the fair. Gretchen and Destiny went and grabbed the tickets for everyone.

Five minutes later, It looked like everyone got their tickets and entered inside. The fair decorations were beautiful.

Layla loved the lights, and she even asked her grandma Gretchen if she could play with the other children.

Destiny wasn't so sure she wanted Layla to run along and play. But then, Gretchen reassured her daughter that she would be fine.

She is a six-year-old girl. I think she should enjoy her childhood as much as she can. Destiny sighs and thinks about how much time she missed being away from her daughter. Gretchen tells her not to think negatively and let go of the past. Gretchen wants her daughter destiny to enjoy time with her daughter Layla. Gretchen understands how Destiny feels; Kaiser robbed Destiny of four years spent with her daughter and the time she could have spent with her daughter.

One of Kaiser's men locked her away when Layla was three years old. Destiny wasn't a teenager when she was kidnapped because Destiny had her daughter at nineteen, and her age at the kidnapping would be twenty-two.

The whole time she has been talking, Gretchen keeps reminding herself that she doesn't want to discuss this. Gretchen wanted to enjoy time at the fair with Destiny and Layla and Elena, Mariah, and Kayla. The girls decide to get ice cream, taking little Lia with them.

Kids play around, eat good food, watch puppet shows, and play games. The ladies loved being around little Layla, and she was such a ball of energy. The ladies even played a game and won her a stuffed toy. Kayla gave it to Layla, and she thanked her very much. Layla's manors were incredible, and she got them from her grandma Gretchen. Many hours went by with every resident in town enjoying their time. The night went on until 10:00 pm, and everyone started departing.

Elena, Mariah, and Kayla walked to Gretchen and told her they would leave. Gretchen gave the ladies a big hug, and off they went. Gretchen takes her daughter destiny and

Layla back to the vehicle as well. Everyone wanted to call it a night.

The following week, Elena, Mariah, and Kayla were busy getting things organized at home. They decided to do some cleaning up of their place. Elena has come downstairs to pick up her mail, and she receives a letter the next thing you know. The letter invited her to a local church reception for the survivors. Kayla and Tori just finished shopping and are on their way home. They also received a letter asking them to attend the church reception on Sunday. There had been an unfortunate incident that had taken place. A public celebration was held in honour of the four survivors. The whole festival was planned by Gretchen Wellsford and a group of community organizers. To Jalen and Aiden, each of the boys was also invited to the commemorative event. As well as Destiny, her granddaughter Layla was also invited. Everyone in the community, Elena, Mariah, and Kayla, wanted to move on from the unfortunate event. They wanted to show their support for the community.

On the following day, the celebration at the church begins. We can see that a car is approaching the church's parking lot. After coming out of their vehicles, the families of the survivors start to make their way into the church. There is a celebration in the downstairs hall of the church. In the vestibule below, many visitors and friends of the community have gathered. The first table had Elena,

Mariah, and Kayla, who sat down. Gretchen Destiny and Layla were seated at the second table. Kayla wondered where the boys were, and she called Jalen. Jalen picks up the phone and tells Kayla that he's there in the parking lot. Within a few minutes, the boys had entered the downstairs hall and sat down at the girls' table. There was a lot of staring going on in the room as the priest walked through the aisle. The priest walks up to the microphone and begins to speak. At the start of his speech, the priest offered some prayers, which were listened to by everyone. Then he called on Gretchen Wellsford, the community organizer, and asked her to speak a few words. The families of each survivor took the stage to say thank you to the community for its support and effort. It was also noteworthy that one of the community organizers, Jill Asher, walked up to the platform and said a few words. Following that, there was a brief pause in which Gretchen Wellsford called upon the lady survivors, one by one.

Firstly, Elizabeth Meadows, a twenty-four-year-old girl with a calm and loving nature, will speak. Following her will be Ariel Molley, a twenty-three-year-old girl with timid and wise qualities, next up, Jenny Noel, twenty-five, is a bright, shy and kind person then we have Destiny Meyer, twenty-two years old, sweet, kind girl and Sky Marshall, a twenty-five-year-old with a bright and gentle personality will follow her. In addition to their lovely dresses, the girls are all wearing pretty accessories. They spoke and expressed their appreciation to the community for helping them locate them. As the survivors finished their speech, they walked to their table in the front row and sat down. Everyone had food and beverages to drink. They talked together, laughed, and shared many memories. It seemed as if the hours of the day flew by very quickly. It was near the end of the celebration, and everyone was getting ready to leave the church.

CHAPTER 17

The summer season has finally arrived in Craven Heights. As the sun shines, the birds are chirping, and it is lovely to be outdoors. Children are playing in the yard. Craven Heights appeared to be a dark, gloomy town in the past. However, that has changed now. There is finally hope once again in a city that has lost its way. There is a feeling of unity amongst the people of a town struggling for a long time. There is even a desire to elect the next mayor a second time. Just a moment later, at the city hall, a black limo arrives, and a woman steps out of it. The woman appeared in her mid-thirties, tall, with black hair and an average build. Upon entering the building, she seemed to be very friendly. As soon as she walks up to the front desk, she lets the receptionist know she has an appointment with the city council. Upon entering the room, she was escorted by Aster Baylor; she is a twenty-one-year-old woman who is considerate and thoughtful. Three council board members greet her. After the woman has seated herself, she introduces herself as Ginger Kats. She is a thirty-eight-year-old woman who is mature and determined in her line of work. Ginger has a warm complexion and wears a blue and black outfit. As the woman is seated, she introduces herself as Ginger Kats. She is a thirty-eight-year-old woman who is mature and quite determined in her line of work. Ginger also has a warm skin tone, is wearing a blue and black outfit, and has long dark red hair.

Members then asked her what brought her to the meeting today. As Ginger explains, she is interested in running for Mayor of Craven Heights. The club members look at each other and secretly discuss what they will accomplish with Ginger. She explains the work she intends to do for this small town. As Ginger explained, she has a master's degree in social studies, is a team player, and has worked as a teaching assistant with colleges and universities. It is no secret that Ginger knows how much a Mayor should accomplish for his town. She explained that she would work with local employers to engage them and work with college leaders and workforce boards to create policies that would bring education programs in line with the demand for talent. Ginger Kats appears to be very interested in the job. Of course, hearing about the crimes committed by former Mayor Kaiser Beckett, she believes many people in the community need support, and the victims' families need help. During her remarks, she also mentioned that she would work with city staff to develop and implement future educational and job training programs within the community. As Mayor of a city, Ginger believes that you need to wake up every day to do your job and be there for your communities. She states that this town has been through quite a bit. Following Ginger's lengthy speech to the council, the council members talked among themselves and said they would decide on the matter at the end of the month. We must work together with the people in our communities. As residents of Craven Heights, they have to know what they are looking for in their next Mayor. Meanwhile, all of this is happening at the same time. The girls were watching the news at home and saw on tv that the reporters were talking about whom the next Mayor would be and where you could go to sign up if you wanted to become the next Mayor.

Elena remarked that it would be cool if Aiden ran for mayor; Aiden just laughed. But Aiden was not interested in running for mayor. Elena was amusing Aiden while they were talking. However, the funny part is that Elena daydreamed about Aiden becoming a city mayor. After that, Aiden told Elena to stop thinking like that. She considered what abilities Aiden might bring to the position of Mayor. As she continued to speak to Aiden, Elena mentioned the money he would be getting if he ran for mayor. Aiden thought about it for a moment before he started to think of what the council would do in hiring a nineteen-year-old college man as a candidate for mayor. Elena explained how cute Aiden was and that all the girls would gush over him. Despite Elena's gratitude, Aiden explained that his high school grades weren't good, and he isn't even from this town.

On the other hand, his college record is excellent. As a result, Aiden declines to run for Mayor. Elena was merely playing a trick on him.

Elena appears to have been pulling his leg and joking around with him. Several people like Ginger Kats signed up to run for the mayor position at the city hall. Ginger Kats was not the only candidate running for the job. A man named Xavier Moore, a thirty-seven-year-old man who has a selfish and curious nature wanted to run for the office of Mayor of Craven Heights. Next, we have Nadir Lennox, a 29-year-old with high energy and wisdom. Finally, Emmanuel Corbin a thirty-three-year-old who has a wealth of skills and knowledge. All of the candidates had many important issues to share with the community. Each had its plan to share with the district. There were some nasty people and some who were friendly and polite. Many people in town were eagerly awaiting to see who the next mayor would be. Three weeks had passed, and everyone in town had voted for their favourite candidate. Polling places were going to be at the local schools. Elena, Mariah, and Kayla go to one of the schools and cast their votes.

Meanwhile, Gretchen and her two daughters had just finished shopping and were about to go to the nearest school to cast their vote. After the vote, the girls met up with Gretchen, and Gretchen explained that her daughter Destiny had never liked Ginger. As it turns out, Ginger attended the same high school as Destiny. It would appear that the two never got along. During her time in high school, Ginger was the most popular girl in class, and she overshadowed other students' lives. Destiny thinks Ginger's running for Mayor of Craven Heights must be a joke. They agreed that Ginger Kats had been cruel to them even though they had not met her personally; it seemed as though she was a wicked person. As a result, they understood why destiny was acting this way. After only a short time here, Destiny and the girls became close friends. The girls were very fond of Destiny. A short while later, the girls were at home watching the news.

Suddenly the news came on, and it looked like the voting polls had closed. Everyone was in their homes waiting for the result. Ginger Kats is at her house in Craven Heights, and so are Xavier Moore, Nadir Lennox, and Emmanuel Corbin. Several news reporters are in the surrounding area. The residents of the town are eagerly awaiting the results. Five minutes later, the results were in, and it appeared that Ginger Kats had won the election. It is safe to say that the moment Destiny heard that on the news, she freaked out. At the same time, Elena, Mariah, and Kayla were also shocked. Gretchen told Destiny to calm down. Reporters surround ginger Kats and the rest of the candidates' homes from the media. There has been a report that Ginger Kats has been elected Mayor of the city and will be addressing the public shortly.

The following day arrives, and it's 10:00 pm in Craven Heights. Now that Ginger Kats has been elected Mayor, she will address the public.

There is an enormous crowd outside as Ginger Kats walks up the stage. Ginger begins her speech by thanking the group and everyone who voted. Ginger also detailed what she has planned as Mayor of Craven Heights. She speaks for Twenty Minutes. As this was happening, people in the crowd were cheering for Ginger Kats. Ginger continues to talk about any upcoming or past issues. She then answers a few questions from the public and reporters. After twenty minutes, she ends the speech and is escorted out through the back of the room. During that time, reporters interviewed former candidates. First, we have Xavier Moore, then we have Nadir Lennox, and finally, we have Emmanuel Corbin. All of them were dressed in a variety of casual and formal clothes. There wasn't much they had to say, but they did detail what they could have done if they were voted into office. Though it is too late, the town has spoken, and they chose Ginger Kats as their Mayor. As the month passes, and it is July 2021, Ginger Kats has already served in the office for two months, and she has already accomplished a lot. One of the things she worked on was developing community workforces. Ginger Kats spoke about the possibility of opening new colleges and universities in Craven Heights. Despite the smaller size of Craven Heights, there is only one local community college, so the town belongs to a small community Ginger Kat's opinion, colleges should be built in the community and accessible to all. Ginger also intends to work with police, fire, housing, and transportation departments.

Ginger Kats is raising the price of education, transportation, and housing. She even understands the Mayor's responsibilities and would be happy to undergo the duties. Ginger even mentions travel destinations. She wants to see more roadways, highways, and bus stations for the town's people. These things would cost a lot of money and hard work by the town's residents.

In comparison, all of this news is coming to light. People in town don't understand what's going on and why Ginger is enforcing these rules. The question lies, is she being forced to make these rules?! She made it mandatory for children to wear uniforms in all schools across town. Ginger is getting tough on everything; she is very strict and wastes time.

Meanwhile, in Craven Heights, ordinary people are heading to work. The city's schools are closed during the summer, but Ginger wants to open the school in August. Parents are not happy about this news, and they think what Ginger is doing is ridiculous. Meanwhile, while this is happening, Gretchen is at work at the library and hears the commotion going on outside. As she exits, she walks to the door and opens it.

There are protestors and people on the street protesting Ginger Kats. Gretchen calls Destiny to tell her what is happening; Destiny already knows what's going on. She arrives at her daughter's school. The school wants to open in August instead of September, and many parents protest that. Destiny knew what a disaster Ginger would bring if she were elected because of the state that is happening now. Gretchen ends the call and rushes back to the library to finish one last-minute work.

After finishing, Gretchen heads out of the library, closes the door, and locks it. Gretchen makes her way to Elena and Mariah's apartment. She stops by her house to grab a few things and then heads there. Gretchen makes it to Elena and Mariah's place. Gretchen knocks on their door, and Mariah opens it. Mariah invites Gretchen in and tells her Elena will be out for a while; she is just getting ready. Gretchen says no problem and waits on the sofa. Mariah offers Gretchen a snack or a drink. Gretchen politely approves. Mariah gives her a sweet mango drink. Gretchen loved the glass; it tasted delicious. Elena finishes getting ready and walks out of the bedroom into the living room. Gretchen welcomes her with a big hug. Elena wondered why she didn't bring Layla with her. Gretchen explained that her daughter Layla was with her mother Destiny and walked to the school about summer break. Elena sighs and remembers she heard on the news that Ginger Kats is changing the rules of summer.

Elena thought it was not very good, but what can you do? Elena explained; that the town already had one psycho Mayor; we don't want another psycho in our hands. Mariah and Gretchen agree with what Elena is saying.

Meanwhile, Kayla and Tori are grocery shopping for the weekend across town. It just so happens that Elena's birthday is coming up and that Jalen Archwood is coming to town with Aiden as a surprise for Elena's birthday. Elena and Mariah have no clue Kayla is planning this surprise party with Jalen and Aiden.

CHAPTER 18

The travel bus arrived in Craven Heights at approximately 6:00 pm; Jalen and Aiden stepped out. They grab their luggage and call Kayla. Kayla answers the phone and tells them to meet at the station's back. Kayla pulls up, parks two seconds later and tells Jalen and Aiden to get in the car. Jalen and Aiden throw their luggage in the back of the vehicle. Then as you know it, the team drives off to Kayla and Tori's apartment. Jalen and Aiden will be staying with Kayla. There are two rooms, so girls in one room and boys in another. Although Jalen and Kayla are a couple, they won't be sleeping together this time. The other room would have Tori and Aiden sleeping together, and Tori doesn't want that to happen.

She knows Elena has a secret crush on Aiden, so she doesn't want to intrude. Kayla thought that was sweet of Tori.

The sleeping arrangements were typically acceptable. Meanwhile, back at Elena and Mariah's apartment, the girls are getting ready to head out to the gallery. It's been weeks since they had even been to the gallery; they had a lot of work to do that day, especially since Derek and Clare almost took the gallery from right under Mariah. After Derek's arrest, he wouldn't be bothering Mariah with anything. So Mariah wasn't so scared to continue improving her gallery with the help of Elena. Kayla texts Mariah about the surprise party and informs them that Jalen and Aiden are in town. Mariah can't keep secrets; that is how she is as a person. She sucks at keeping secrets, but Kayla told her to keep this one. It was important for Mariah to keep this secret because they wanted to surprise their best friend Elena on her birthday. They remember last year's birthday when Elena struggled in Sunsfield while her dad tremendously drank till he couldn't control his behaviour. So Kayla needed to throw Elena a surprise birthday party. Kayla wanted to show how much friendship means to her. Kayla texts Mariah to distract Elena for the whole afternoon while Kayla, Aiden, Jalen, and Tori decorate the apartment. The party will be at Kayla and Tori's apartment. Jalen and Aiden will get drinks and snacks while Kayla and Tori decorate the entire place with streamers and balloons.

Back at the gallery, Mariah is getting nervous while distracting Elena. Does Elena wonder what is wrong with Mariah today? Elena brushes it off and continues to do some work around the gallery. Just then, Mariah's phone beeped, and it was Kayla again. Kayla informed Mariah that everything was okay with taking Elena to the apartment by text message. So Mariah told Elena she was going to close up early today. Elena didn't wonder why, but she said okay, cleaned up her desk, and walked to the door to close up, but Mariah beat her. Elena didn't know what was wrong with Mariah. As it has been said before, Mariah can't keep secrets. This secret was eating her alive. Mariah then tells her she needs to change her clothes. Elena thought something was off with Mariah. Elena nervously agreed. Elena and Mariah head over to her apartment and change clothes. Elena took forever to change, she didn't know what to wear, and she also didn't know where Mariah was taking her.

For all we know, she may be kidnapping her. All jokes aside, Mariah and Elena make it to Kayla and Tori's apartment. Mariah and Elena find a good parking spot, hop out of the car, and walk to the building entrance.

Still, Elena doesn't know why they are all dressed up to go to Kayla and Tori's apartment. Kayla buzzes them up; Mariah tells Elena to follow her and close her eyes. At the building entrance, Mariah presses the buzzer number. Elena stops in her tracks and wonders why she has to close her eyes. Mariah just told her to do it. Elena closes her eyes and walks with Mariah to the door.

The door opens, and everybody yells, "Surprise" Elena is so speechless by all her friends being there that Kayla runs up to Elena and hugs her. Moments later, Aiden and Jalen go up to Elena and hug her. Elena is surprised to see both her best friends, Aiden and Jalen. Elena had no clue they were there. Then comes Gretchen Wellsford, her daughter Destiny, and Layla. Little Layla wishes Elena a happy birthday and gives her a present. The birthday party went on for hours and hours, and there was some delicious food, cake, music, games, and much more. You would expect the landlord to kick a bunch of party-goers out, but he didn't. The neighbours were pretty cool and polite people. They didn't complain at all. The night of the party then ends, and everyone decides to leave. Elena makes a little speech thanking everyone who came to her birthday and her new friends for planning it. It was a long night; Elena and Mariah said bye to everyone as they left. Kayla and Tori stay behind and clean up the place. Jalen and Aiden go outside for a smoke. Jalen then starts talking to Aiden, much more serious about the whole situation with Elena. Jalen wonders why Aiden didn't move Elena at her birthday party.

Aiden explained that he didn't want to move so fast because he was nervous. The plan was that Aiden would come to Craven Heights for Elena's birthday, surprise her, and tell Elena how he felt about her. The program went as planned, and the party was a hit, but Aiden didn't tell Elena anything. I guess he chickened out. Jalen tells Aiden to find the courage and tell her before leaving town in two days. Aiden and Jalen will leave in two days, and Aiden doesn't tell Elena how he feels about her. So Aiden decides to call Mariah and ask for her advice.

Mariah answers the phone, and they talk for a bit of bit until Aiden tries to spill the secrets. Mariah tries to tell Aiden no more secrets and that she can't take any more secrets, and Aiden starts laughing. Mariah hangs up the phone quickly, then texts Aiden to stop whatever he does. Aiden then explained; that he wanted to tell Elena how he felt about her.

Mariah couldn't stop screaming in her sleep. She wanted to text Elena right away, but she knew she couldn't. Aiden wants one of the girls to help him, and he is only close to Kayla, Mariah, and of course, Elena. So either

Mariah helps him or Kayla helps him. Two days earlier, Aiden decides to go to the flower shop, pick up some flowers and a card, and then go to Elena's apartment. Previously Aiden told Mariah to get out of the apartment, so she did. Aiden decided to work with Mariah on this plan. Kayla is at her new job that day, and Elena is at home organizing her clothes and doing housework stuff. Mariah told Elena to work from home that day. So that is what Elena did.

Hours later, Aiden arrives at Elena and Mariah's apartment. Mariah isn't there, but Elena is. Aiden nervously knocks on the door. Elena answers it. She isn't surprised to see Aiden; she tells him to come in. Elena asks if he wants anything to drink or eat. Aiden nods and agrees to something to drink. Of course, Elena gives him the sweetest mango juice. So then Aiden sat down with Elena on the couch. He finally decides to tell her how he feels about her. It has been a long time since August 2019 since Aiden felt this way about Elena. He had to get it off his chest whether she liked him or not. So he blurts it out. Elena's eyes bulge out. She doesn't know what to say exactly; she gets up, walks to the corner of the room, and starts whispering to herself. Aiden walks up to her and tries to hear what she is talking about. Elena puts both her hands on her mouth. Aiden wants Elena to say something, anything. So she does; Elena explains that she tried to tell Aiden how she felt one year ago but didn't think he felt the same way.

Aiden's eyes open wide, and then he starts to laugh. Elena wonders why he is laughing. I guess it was just a nervous laugh. A lot of people get that. Aiden tells her to sit down and talk about it. Elena sits down beside Aiden, and they talk for hours.

Meanwhile, Mariah is at Kayla's apartment. Jalen watches a sports game, and Kayla fights Jalen over the remote. While that was happening, Elena and Aiden stopped talking, and they looked into the eyes of each other and shared a passionate kiss. Following the kiss, they headed to Kayla and Tori's house, where everyone was, and shared the good news with everyone. Elena and Aiden were finally together. All their friends were happy for them. Two days after Aiden and Jalen leave town, Elena, Mariah, and Kayla return to their lives in Craven Heights. Elena and Mariah travelled to the gallery to design more artwork; Kayla started a new writing job at Vison Media Centre. She even paid Jalen a loan that she received from him. Tori returns to being a dispatcher.

Gretchen, her daughter Destiny, and granddaughter Layla move to a new house in town. Jalen and Aiden have returned to Port Sunfield, and they are preparing themselves to live as roommates, ready for the last year of their engineering program and find a place to live on their own. Mayor Ginger Kats steps into the Mayor's office. It is her first day on the job, she puts in motion the plan to reopen all schools in August. Consequently, Craven Heights and Port Sunfield are expected to have a wonderful summer.

CPSIA information can be obtained
at www.ICGtesting.com
Printed in the USA
LVHW100114250922
729205LV00022B/507

9 781685 833121